How could Millicent choose...?

"I love you, Millicent." His breath was warm in her hair. "Could you ever love a sober old man like me?"

Laughter bubbled up in her and filled the room. She took his lean, bearded face between her hands. "Could I ever? Why Adam, I've loved you almost since we met."

She watched joy follow disbelief across his face, and then he caught her so tightly to him that she gasped. He loosened his hold immediately, looking stricken, and she snuggled against his chest to reassure him. She shouldn't be with him like this, not when she couldn't commit to spending her life with him. Yet surely a few minutes in his arms couldn't hurt. "With eyes that speak as eloquently as yours, you could never be an old man, Adam."

His fingers played with the curls at the back of her neck, sending shivers of delight through her, and his soft beard caressed her temple. "And have you heard those eyes ask whether you will marry me, Millicent Strong?"

JOANN A. GROTE feels strongly that fiction has an important place in spreading God's message of salvation and encouraging Christians to become more like Christ. *The Unfolding Heart* is her second *Heartsong Presents* novel.

Books by JoAnn A. Grote

HP36—The Sure Promise

The Unfolding Heart

JoAnn A. Grote

A Sequel to *The Sure Promise*

Heartsong Presents

Dedicated with love to my parents,
Audrey Fall Olsen and James S. "Dugie" Olsen.

ISBN 1-55748-442-2

THE UNFOLDING HEART

PRINTED IN THE U.S.A.

To the Reader

Chippewa City still exists in western Minnesota, though it is called by another name, as it was in 1878. This is a love story, however, not a history. I have attempted to make the background authentic, but the active characters are fictional. The names of a few actual local persons are mentioned, but these are not active characters: Mr. and Mrs. Moyer, Mr. Frink, and Nettie Bartlett. The editor's advertisement for a school ma'am and the school ma'am's response did appear in *The Lac Qui Parle Press*, a newspaper published only a few miles from Chippewa City; I modified the letters only slightly for the purposes of my story. The incident of the older boys repairing the schoolhouse actually took place in a county adjoining Chippewa County, as related in the *History of Chippewa and Lac Qui Parle Counties* by Moyer and Dayle.

The present site of Chippewa City is a lovely town, filled with stately trees, many of which were planted by the early settlers. The area's farms are rich and fertile. If they could see Chippewa County today, the old settlers would be proud.

JoAnn A. Grote

"Why I *never*!" Millicent Strong jumped up from the emerald brocade loveseat and crossed the parlor, indignation in every step. Her blue eyes snapped as she shook the small newspaper beneath her landlady's nose. "Just look at this, Mrs. Canfield. Look what the *Valley Ventilator* has printed now."

With her usual calm, gray-haired Mrs. Canfield laid the lace she was crocheting on the marble-topped, rosewood table beside her chair. "I trust the article is not about Doctor Strong, Millicent." Her round hands reached for the small frontier newspaper. "I cannot imagine your brother doing anything so outrageous that its advertisement would anger you."

"Of course he wouldn't." Millicent flipped a long blonde curl over her shoulder. "The only outrageous thing my brother ever did was move to Chippewa City on that forsaken Minnesota frontier. You'd think an educated man could find a more civilized place to live in 1878."

"Moving to the frontier was not outrageous, dear. Doctor Strong believed he was following God's call for his life. There is a difference, you know."

Millicent didn't know any such thing. As much as she loved her brother, she'd never understood his belief that God took a personal interest in his life. She did know the folly of trying to change Mrs. Canfield's mind, though, but she couldn't resist one last argument. "Doctors are needed in cities, also, and nearby Chicago is certainly more civilized than that group of buildings he calls a town." Before the older woman could respond, Millicent pointed a slim finger to the article she'd been reading. "Just read the ad the editor's written, Mrs. Canfield."

She watched as Mrs. Canfield held the paper at arm's length, tilting her head this way and that to focus the words. "'School ma'ams are scarce in this county,'" she read aloud in her slow, well-modulated voice. "'Any young lady, twenty-one years of age, with a capital of two or three hundred dollars, would do well here. She could preempt a quarter section of land, teach school all summer, and get married in the fall. Fact!'

"Hmmm." Mrs. Canfield lifted her snowy brows to peer over the top of her sewing glasses at Millicent. "Are you thinking of accepting his challenge?"

"Accepting. . .!" Shock strangled her sputter. "Of course not! Teach on that wild wasteland? I'd rather . . .rather. . .spend my life in abject poverty."

"Mmmm." Mrs. Canfield handed the paper back to Millicent and reached for her lacework. "A shame. Sounds like just the place for you."

"Mrs. Canfield!"

"Well, you are a school teacher, dear. One of the best, if I do say so myself, having assisted in your training. I was proud to have you replace me when I retired." The needles stilled as she lowered her work to her ample lap and pinned Millicent with a deliberate look. "You have been living with me since your parents died when you were fifteen. You are like family to me, especially with Mr. Canfield dead these ten years. But you are twenty-one years old, and it is time you married and started a family of your own."

Millicent propped tiny fists on the blue basque that flared over her hips. "Are you trying to get rid of me, Mrs. Canfield?" She filled her voice with indignation.

The older woman shook a plump finger at her. "I see the laughter in those dark blue eyes, Millicent Strong. But I say again, it is time you married. It stands to reason the frontier has its share of single men—real men, eager to face whatever the world might throw at them. After all, it takes strong people to build a new land."

Millicent crossed her arms over her ribbon-trimmed bodice. "We've had enough discussions on women's rights to assure me you agree that a woman no longer needs a man to take care of her."

"I'm not referring to leaning on a man. I'm speaking of loving and being loved."

"Should I decide I need a young man for *any* reason, I know more than enough men right here in Illinois, thank you." Millicent softened her statement with a smile.

"Pooh!" Mrs. Canfield dismissed Millicent's suitors with a wave of her hand. "I never did like that Mr. Thomas Wilcox that hangs around you. He is too pompous to be any use to the world at all. And Mr. Terrence Bradford, well, he is afraid of his own shadow."

Millicent lowered herself to the serpentine-backed loveseat, her grin fading. "You never told me you felt that way about my escorts."

"You are old enough to know your own mind, Millicent. Besides, I have not as yet met any young men that appear to be better candidates for matrimony than those two specimen."

Millicent struggled to restrain a laugh. Imagine Thomas

Wilcox's consternation if he heard himself referred to as a specimen!

Mrs. Canfield pointed a needle toward the settlement newspaper. "But this land, well, it sounds full of men worthy of an intelligent, high-spirited lass like yourself."

Embarrassment prodded Millicent to rise and move hastily toward the entryway. "As if I want to spend my life with a cowboy or a sod-buster!" she tossed over her shoulder. "I'm going to write a letter to that foolish editor and tell him just what a proper young lady thinks of his invitation!" She hurried up the stairs as fast her slim skirt allowed.

Seated by a small table in her room, inkwell and writing paper before her, Millicent's mind drifted back over her conversation with Mrs. Canfield. A sigh escaped her as she rested her chin in her palm and stared out the window, tree limbs and rooftops filling her view. She agreed with Mrs. Canfield that there were no good prospects for marriage in the vicinity, none of her acquaintance, at least. But then, her standards were high. The man she could love completely would have to measure up to her brother, Dr. Matthew Strong.

Loneliness slipped over her like a soft gray mist. She hadn't seen Matthew in three years, but she could still picture his broad face, the laughing blue eyes so much like her own, as he waved goodbye from the train. When almost out of sight, he'd whipped the hat from his blonde hair and waved it furiously over his head. She'd hardly been able to see through her tears.

Her fingers played with her own blonde curls as she examined her memories. Matthew had been in his first year at Rush Medical School when their parents' buggy was struck by a train at a crossing during a thunderstorm, killing them both. Matthew had spoken to her instructor, Mrs. Canfield, after the funeral, and arranged for Millicent to board with the widow while she finished her schooling. Chicago wasn't far, and he often made the trip late Saturday afternoon to spend Sundays with her. Millicent had lived for those Sundays.

They went faithfully to church with Mrs. Canfield each week. Millicent never told either of them that she didn't believe in the God they worshipped, though she did try to live her life by the moral principles the church taught. But in the lives of the people she saw everyday, she saw little evidence of the God spoken of in the pastor's Bible-readings. She just couldn't bring herself to believe that seeing God in the here-after was more important than seeing God in the present.

Of course, one couldn't help but see Matthew's and Mrs. Canfield's faith reflected in their lives, Millicent's honest nature forced her to admit, but they were exceptions.

"It stands to reason the frontier has its share of men— real men," Mrs. Canfield had said. Could the frontier possibly hold more men who were fine and upright like Matthew? What a useless thought! She wasn't about to leave the comfort of civilization to discover whether Mrs. Canfield's conjecture was correct.

She touched her pen to the paper. "To the Editor of the *Valley Ventilator*. Greeting."

Reverend Adam Conrad stepped from Chippewa City's muddy main street into the town's only general store. Bright prairie sun poured through the windows, exposing the vast array of goods which filled every inch of the narrow building's walls.

Two older men were playing chess beside the pot-bellied stove in the middle of the room. Although the calendar nailed to the wall read April twelfth, no fire burned in the stove; the spring was mild this year for Minnesota. The strong smell of pickled fish rose from the barrel beside the door, and Adam moved quickly into the building away from the doorway.

"Howdy, Reverend."

Adam touched a hand to the brim of his black hat and nodded to the course young man in the worn flannel shirt and patched trousers. "Charley. I see you've shaved off that tough red beard."

Charley tipped back the barrel on which he was seated. With his spine resting against a post, he shifted his cigar from one side of his mouth to the other, then clamped down on the brown stub and grinned. "Yup. Spring is here, and I figure to do some courtin'. Better think about gettin' rid of your own bush, Reverend. I hear tell the ladies like men clean shaven these days."

Adam felt color drain from the lean face his trim black beard partially covered, and his jaw tightened. Was Charley's statement a thinly disguised jest at the fact that Laurina Dalen, the woman he'd been engaged to marry until two weeks ago, was to marry clean-shaven Matthew Strong on Sunday? His eyes bored into Charley's, but he could see no trace of meanness. "Think I'll keep my beard a while yet," he said mildly. He moved past Charley to locate his purchase, and Charley gave his attention to the newspaper balancing on his lap.

A moment later a chuckle sprang from Charley's throat. In an instant it grew to a belly laugh, and Charley had to grab his cigar stub to keep from choking on it. "Hoo-ey! Has this little lady given our editor a piece of her tongue! Listen to this, men.

"'To the Editor of the *Valley Ventilator*. Greeting. You advertise for a school ma'am. A young lady who has reached the age of twenty-one, with a capital of two or three hundred dollars, can, by coming to your village, have the extreme pleasure of preempting a quarter section of land, teaching school, and then getting married. Just think of it!

"'I wonder whose the land would be after the ceremony? I wonder if it would be a town site? I wonder if there would be time to raise corn for the winter's provision? (I believe they raise corn on new breaking if the grasshoppers are merciful?) I wonder if the young gentlemen have already flirted with all the young ladies in the county? I wonder if ours would be a sod house?

"'Well never mind, there is a surplus of school ma'ams in our state, extra No.1 school ma'ams, and the time in which to dispose of them has come. I think they are on an average twenty-one years of age, handsome, entertaining and agreeable, unsurpassed in all the accomplishments of the modern age.

"'As to the two or three hundred dollars, I can't say. They, judging from my own case, wouldn't hesitate to borrow under such circumstances.

"'Really now, all the beautiful surroundings—the sunny extended plateau, where barks the nimble gopher, or feeds the voracious grasshopper, the silvery lakes and rivers, the haunts of the wild fowl and fish—must afford pleasant facilities for hunting and fishing (the usual pastime of young ladies).

"'The health and vivacity which comes from recreations, truly make up an almost irresistible invitation to come and spend a vacation at least.

"'And who would stop to talk of trees when they could buy a farm with room to plant a million such?

"'So I don't know but that instead of one, you may look for a bevy of school ma'ams, equipped with birch canoes, hunting pouches, rifles, revolvers and bowie knives, apparelled in kirtle and girdle, like the "maid who walks in the morning shod like a mountaineer."

"'You have promised us an escort; there must be more than one else we should audibly disagree, which would be rather at variance with our dignity.

"'Who would go for recreation to the cities of the east when such inducements are held forth on the frontier?' Signed, 'School Ma'am.'"

Guffaws and cheers from the store clerk and the chess players accompanied Charley's melodramatic reading. Reverend Adam Conrad stood beside the shelves at the back of the store and let a smile slide across his face. The letter was amusing, but he admired the girl's spirit. He'd seen too many women nimbly change their opinions to please their most recent suitor—no wonder so many men awoke after their wedding to a different woman than they thought they'd married. The man who married this school ma'am would have only himself to blame if he didn't know her well.

Charley was still wiping tears of laughter from his eyes as Adam laid thirty cents on the counter, picked up the gallon jug of kerosene oil for his lamp, and started back into the morning sunshine.

On impulse he stopped further along the straggling main

street at the tiny log house that served as both the news office of the *Valley Ventilator* and the editor's home. Wouldn't hurt to see what other news there was in the paper, he told himself.

But when he reached his three-room clapboard house on the edge of the prairie, it wasn't the rest of the newspaper he read. Instead, he turned to the letter the School Ma'am had written. This time he read it slowly against the backdrop of the meadowlark's song rather than the irreverent laughter of the men at the store.

He leaned against the door jamb when he finished, letting the cool winds wash over him with the scent of new prairie grass. As his gaze roamed over the treeless plateau, he found himself strangely drawn toward the unknown woman. Foolishness! He shook his head. Even if he knew her, she wouldn't be interested in him. He wasn't vain; he knew well enough that women didn't find his quiet, reserved manner attractive.

Perhaps he was just trying to replace Laurina in his heart. After all, only two weeks ago he had freed her from their engagement. This Sunday she would wed Dr. Matthew Strong, his closest friend.

Since the broken engagement, invisible bands had bound his chest, and now they tightened. He was almost growing accustomed to the pain of loneliness, the sense of something precious lost that filled his heart every waking moment since saying goodbye to Laurina.

Not that Adam would change things. Laurina and Matthew loved each other, and regardless of his own regret, Adam was sure God wanted them together.

"You have no reason to feel sorry for yourself, Adam Conrad," he reminded himself. "You were the one who broke the engagement, not Laurina." She'd never spoken to him of her love for Matthew, but Adam had seen the way they looked at each other, felt the tension between them. Adam swallowed the lump that filled his throat. He couldn't hold her to her promise to marry him when he realized the deep love she and Matthew shared. "Help me, Lord," he said softly into the breeze. "Help me not to covet my friend's wife."

Laurina had argued with him when he offered to release her from the engagement, insisting she respected him and would learn to love him. As if he wanted a wife who would *learn* to care for him! Adam had told her not to concern herself about him, that God had someone else for him—someplace. He was trying hard to remember that. But already he missed Laurina, and the two abandoned children she was raising, Johnny and Pearl.

For the children's sake Laurina and Matthew were marrying so soon after she and Adam had broken their engagement—but it was still hard on Adam's pride to face the townspeople, wondering what they were thinking behind their smiles. Part of him wanted to run, to leave behind the settlement and people who knew of his engagement. But he'd sworn himself to the Lord's service, and the Lord, and not his smarting pride, must direct his actions.

If he was squarely honest with himself, perhaps he missed the children more than he missed Laurina. Just remembering their faces squeezed his heart. Even now, he could feel three-year-old Pearl's chubby little arms around his neck. He sighed, longing for a family of his own.

"Delight thyself also in the Lord; and he shall give thee the desires of thine heart." Psalm 37 rang through his mind and eased the pain that filled his chest. He'd been right to break his engagement with Laurina. In His own time, God would bring Adam the woman He'd chosen for him.

Adam's gaze searched the sky for signs of clouds, and he was relieved to see none. Tomorrow he would drive to Granite Falls to pick up a load of lumber. He'd have to leave at daybreak to make the fifteen mile trip each way and be home by dark. The muscle in his jaw jerked. He'd ordered that lumber when he thought he and Laurina would be married. His home was small, with only a kitchen, sitting room, and one bedchamber, and with the lumber he'd planned to build a lean-to bedchamber for the children. He wouldn't be needing the extra room now.

He looked down at the paper still in his hand. Laurina would never have written such an article. She was too much the proper eastern lady to say such things. Still, beneath the sarcasm of the article, he sensed a strength, the same kind of steel determination he'd seen in quiet Laurina when she'd taken over the care of the children against the advice of the entire community. Too bad the School Ma'am wasn't enticed by the frontier. Chippewa City could use more women like her and Laurina.

Adam folded the paper along the edges of the article and carefully tore it. Ignoring his feelings of juvenile foolishness, he placed the piece of newsprint in the top bureau drawer that held his sermons. A longing as soft as the prairie breeze washed over him. He sure wished he could meet the author of that article.

two

Millicent reached shaking fingers for the wire the delivery boy held out to her. Who might send her a wire except Matthew? Could he have been hurt?

She turned to the marble-topped hall table and with suddenly cold fingers removed a coin for the delivery boy from her black reticule. Taking a deep breath, she unfolded the paper, her fingers fumbling. As she read the words, her breath rushed out in a whoop.

Grabbing up her slender skirt, she hurried to the parlor. "Mrs. Canfield, Matthew is getting married!"

Mrs. Canfield looked up from the book she was reading. Sunlight spilled between green velvet drapes, falling on the tiny lines age had left on her plump cheeks. "Married? To anyone we know?" The rays danced off her spectacles as Millicent ran to her across the flower-patterned carpet.

Millicent's heart warmed to the sincere pleasure that filled Mrs. Canfield's face. She really is like family to me and Matthew, Millicent thought, and we to her. The blonde curls caught high on the back of her head bounced as she shook her head in response to Mrs. Canfield's question. "I don't recognize the name, so he must have met her out West. He says only that he's marrying Miss Laurina Dalen in Chippewa City next Sunday."

"So soon!"

A small frown puckered Mrs. Canfield's thick brows, and doubt touched Millicent's heart. She stomped it out promptly. "Miss Dalen must be a wonderful woman. Matthew is too fine to love any woman but the best."

Mrs. Canfield's age-rounded shoulders straightened. "Yes, of course."

But Millicent saw that doubt lingered in Mrs. Canfield's faded blue eyes. She wondered herself why Matthew was apparently marrying without waiting the proper amount of time. She dropped her gaze to the wire now crushed in her hands. "Next Sunday. How I wish I could be there!"

"And why can't you, pray tell?"

Millicent's lashes flew open in surprise. "I mustn't leave during school term. Who would teach the classes? And it's hundreds of miles to Chippewa City. I'd have to arrange for train passage, and pack, and purchase a wedding gift, and—well, it's just not possible."

Mrs. Canfield slammed her book shut and dropped it on the table beside her. "It is no difficulty to purchase a train ticket or a gift, or to pack. I happen to know you have more than enough money set aside for the cost of the trip. Of course, since you would be unchaperoned, you would need to ride in the Ladies' Car on the train. As to your classes, well, I may be in my dotage, but I guess I can still teach reading, writing, and arithmetic."

"You're far from your dotage." Millicent laughed. "But I couldn't ask you to make such a sacrifice."

"Nonsense." Mrs. Canfield took one of Millicent's slender hands in both her own. Leaning forward, she said earnestly, "You are Matthew's only family, Millicent. You should be at his wedding."

She was right, of course, Millicent thought, and hope put out tenuous roots in her heart. "Do you really think the school board would allow you to substitute for me?" she asked slowly.

Mrs. Canfield dropped Millicent's hand and plopped her own age-freckled hands on her knees. "Mr. Earnest Tuttle is chairman of the school board. It took every teaching trick I knew to get him through the eighth grade. I'd like to see him try to stop me from substituting for you!"

The scent of rosewater surrounded Millicent as she hugged her friend. "I'll do it, Mrs. Canfield. I'll do it!" Her joy bubbled into laughter.

Millicent drew herself to her full five feet two inches and settled an indignant look on the skinny man behind the counter of the small train station in Granite Falls. In her most authoritative teacher's voice, she demanded, "But it is imperative I reach Chippewa City today."

"Like I said, Miss, the stage left for Chippewa City at seven this mornin', four hours ago. T'day's Saturday and the stage won't run ag'in 'til Monday. If yer so all-fired determined ta git there t'day, ya better try the livery down the street. Cain't see why a body'd want ta go ta that good-fer-nothin' excuse fer a town when they kin stay in a fine city like Granite Falls instead." He chuckled at his own humor, and his face folded into a hundred wrinkles. "Next." He waved her out of the way, looking over her head at the man waiting behind her.

Millicent stood her ground. "May I leave my bags here while I search for the livery?"

Bony shoulders lifted a once-white shirt in a shrug. "Suit yerself."

Millicent looked around the busy stationhouse and fought back dismay. Men in every class of dress bustled about the station, jostling one another in their impatience, whether to get a ticket back East or to begin their labors here in the West. Worn, simple clothes were the most common as men came to find new lands. Many of the men in more formal suits and derbies were land speculators. Millicent had learned that much during the long train journey.

She didn't like the appraising looks she received from many of the men. Would her bags be safe here? Noticing a boy loitering outside the station, she paid him to watch her things.

As she walked toward the livery, the sounds of the train station were replaced by the creak and rumble of wagons and the plod, plod of horse hooves on the packed ground of the wide dirt street. Voices of the people she passed surprised her with their many accents and languages, most of which appeared to her inexperienced ear to be Scandinavian.

She was glad she'd worn a dust ruffle beneath her blue traveling suit. Perhaps it would catch the dirt from this uncivilized street.

When she finally reached the livery, the owner was no more help than the stationmaster had been. "Everything with wheels or legs has been rented out for days," he said as they talked in front of the stable's wide door. "What with the early spring, land hunters is everywhere. But I'll be glad to let ya know soon's a buggy comes in. Shouldn't do it, as I've promised others afore ya, but seein' as yer such a pretty thing. . . ," he leered.

She turned her back on him smartly and began to cross the busy street. "I guess I'll find ya at the hotel," he called after her.

Millicent straightened her shoulders, ignoring the

warmth that flooded her neck and face. She hoped no one realized he was directing his words at her. Mrs. Canfield could keep these "real men" of the frontier. How could Matthew stand to live in such a raw land, among uncouth people like the stationmaster and the livery owner?

Surely in this busy place someone could help her reach Chippewa City. After traveling all the way from Illinois, she wasn't going to sit fifteen miles away while Matthew married, she promised herself as she waited impatiently for a wagon to pass.

"Runaways!"

The word that shot terror through the heart of every parent and child broke through the town's noise. Her gaze darted over the crowded street. Where were they? Where were the runaways?

People raced past her, parents pulling children, urging them toward the safety of the buildings. Millicent grabbed up her frock to join them, but the draping across the front of her skirt, caught fashionably behind her knees, hindered her. She stumbled over a rut and struggled for her balance, her satin reticule swinging wildly from her wrist.

Pounding hooves drummed the earthen street; she twisted about to see two horses almost on top of her. Her narrow shoes were rooted to the ground as the bared teeth and wild eyes loomed over her. She could not escape from the path of that huge head!

Suddenly she was yanked aside and thrown to the ground. The breath was knocked from her lungs, and she sensed a heavier body fall between her and the flashing hooves. Hands gripped her arms as the man shielded her from the flying stones.

In an instant that felt as long as her entire life, the horses passed. She looked up to see them still racing down the street, scattering people and horses before them, a driver-less buggy careening behind them. Millicent barely noticed the people rushing toward her and her rescuer as she watched the buggy slam into a hitching rail, smashing the side of the buggy and bringing the horses to a rearing halt.

Gasping to fill her lungs with air, she sat up, her rescuer's hands slipping from her arms. Voices asked whether she was all right, but she could only nod at the faces surrounding her. Someone asked if Adam was hurt, and she realized Adam must be her rescuer's name. He pushed himself to a sitting position, and air rushed into her lungs at last, filling her chest with welcome pain. When they saw that Millicent and the man called Adam were not seriously injured, the strangers drifted away.

Adam got to his feet, pulling her up with him. His hands cupped her shoulders with a steady but gentle touch. "Are you injured, Miss?"

His voice was so deep that its vibrations rumbled through her like the warning tremors before an earth-quake. The eyes looking into her own were almost black, set deep beneath straight black eyebrows. His lean face was white above the beard now filled with dirt from the road.

She shook her head. "No." She forced the quaver from her voice.

"Thank you, Lord." Long lashes swept down, hiding his eyes, and his shoulders sagged with relief. Wonder filled Millicent at the vehemence of his words.

Blood trickled from his face where the road had scraped away a layer of skin. A small cry escaped her, and her gloved hand darted to his cheek, her fingertips resting lightly beside the injury. "You're hurt!"

His eyes flew open at her touch, and he jerked his head back just enough that her fingers fell away, yet his hands remained on her shoulders. "It's only a scratch."

Consternation swept through her as she realized she'd just touched a stranger in the midst of a public street. What must he think of her? "I'm sorry. But you see, no one has ever risked their life for me before," she said.

Something flashed deep in his eyes, and his fingers tightened on her arms as he released a shuddering breath.

"Are you certain you weren't kicked?" she asked, frowning. "The hooves were so close." She blinked away the image of flying legs and feet.

"I'm sure. I'm glad you weren't harmed." She liked the slow way he spoke; his voice was peaceful and reassuring. His gaze dropped to one arm of her dark blue traveling outfit. "I wish I could say as much for your dress."

Millicent brushed at the cloth. "It's not torn—it's only dirty. I will need to clean the soot left from the train, anyway." She looked over her shoulder. "At least my dress is in better shape than that poor buggy. That is one conveyance no one will be using to seek land."

His hands dropped away from her arms, and Millicent was surprised by the regret that rolled over her. He bent to retrieve her hat, and her hands darted to her hair. It had been properly pinned at the back of her head before they fell; now it tumbled free in loose golden curls. She noticed his gaze linger on its length, and she pushed the curls self-consciously behind her shoulders.

He tried to brush dust from her blue hat. Its black satin trim matched the lapels of her basque jacket, but despite his efforts, it was hopelessly smeared now with dust. Millicent forced away the smile that jumped to her lips at his clumsy attempt to clean it. She reached for the hat. "Thank you. And thank you for saving my life."

She gave him her nicest smile, and waited for his answering smile. When it did not come, she turned toward the hotel, saddened. Her heart clamored to stay longer with this man, but she had no excuse to linger. She wished she at least had his smile to take with her.

"Miss—"

"Yes?" She turned eagerly toward him.

"I couldn't help overhearing your discussion with the livery owner. I'm headed to Chippewa City, Miss." He swung the hand holding his own floppy hat toward a wagon filled with lumber. "It wouldn't be a comfortable ride, but if you truly need to reach there today, I'd be pleased to have you join me."

The bright sun shining down could not compare to the sunshine that filled her heart at the chance to spend more time with this man. She knew her smile was far too radiant to bestow on a stranger, but she didn't care. "Sir, you are a true Godsend. You see, my brother is being married tomorrow."

The deep set eyes widened slightly. "Matthew Strong is your brother?"

"Yes. Do you know him?"

"I know him well. I'm Adam Conrad. And you must be Millicent."

She loved hearing him say her name, slowly, the deep voice tumbling across her heart. "You must know him well if you know my name."

"He speaks of you often." The black brows met. "It's

not like Matthew not to meet your train. He must have been called away on an emergency."

"He didn't know I was coming." She smiled ruefully. "I wanted to surprise him."

He nodded seriously, and she was glad neither his eyes nor his voice laughed at her. "It's almost noon," he said. "We'll need to leave within the hour. With the train in and all the land seekers in town, the hotel restaurant will be overflowing, but I know the owner. I'll ask if he'll allow you to use a room to freshen up, and perhaps he'll have the cook put together some lunch for us."

His thoughtfulness touched her. In spite of his sweaty shirt and worn jeans, he was a true gentleman.

I like the way he looks at me, she thought as they walked to collect her valises from the train station. He looks straight into my eyes, one person to another, without the boldness of a flirt, like Thomas Wilcox, or the stifling adoration of Terrence Bradford.

She wondered what Mrs. Canfield would think of him. A smile tugged at her lips. Mrs. Canfield would think he was a "real man."

three

Half an hour later, Adam stuffed her valises and hat boxes in with the lumber and laid a blanket to pad the high wagon seat. He regretted that she'd pinned up her hair again, the curls caught demurely at the back of her head, just below the blue hat that tilted at a beguiling angle over her left ear. Blue stones dangling in silver from her ears caught the sun and winked at him. He thought their color dull next to the blue of Millicent's eyes. He liked the way those eyes met his so openly, with no shyness or flirtation. Her strength of spirit surprised him. Even when she first realized she was safe from the runaways, she didn't collapse in tears or moan over the state of her clothing as so many women would. Instead, her concern had been for him and that minor scratch. His cheek tingled even now at the memory of her touch

When she had looked into his face with her lash-framed eyes wide and said breathlessly, "No one's ever risked their life for me before," he'd had to stop himself from catching her to his chest and touching his lips to those blonde-tipped lashes. The knowledge unnerved him. He'd never reacted so strongly to a woman, not even Laurina.

Perhaps the violent emotions surrounding their unusual meeting were what drew him so to Millicent. Not many people meet each other with possible death only inches away. When he recalled how close she had come to being trampled beneath those hooves, his heart nearly failed him. Thank the Lord, He'd helped him reach her in time.

"Delight thyself also in the Lord; and He shall give thee the desires of thine heart." Why should that verse come to mind again now, he wondered.

His attention was forced back to his driving as he maneuvered around a stump in the middle of the street. Two disheveled men were trying to uproot the stump with shovels. One of them peered up at Millicent from a face thick with stubble and cackled. "Looky here," he called hoarsely to his companion. "A real lady. Why don't ya step down and chat awhile, missy? We could show you a real good time."

Adam urged the horses to quicken their pace, keeping his temper with an effort. As the man's chortles were lost in the jangle of the wagon, Millicent's rounded chin rose an inch and soft color spread over her cheeks.

"I'm sorry you were exposed to that, Miss Strong," Adam said. "Digging stumps from the streets is the sheriff's way of putting men to work who have been jailed for imbibing. Helps the town clear the roads, but it does put unseemly characters in the public's path."

She laughed. "What a novel idea. And does the punishment prevent further indulgence?"

"Not so one would notice, unfortunately. When it comes to saving one from the dangers of drink, Christ is more effective than punishment."

She gave him a startled look, then dropped her gaze to her lap. What had he said to cause such a reaction, he wondered.

"I do believe you rescued me in more ways than one today, Mr. Conrad. You are the only true gentleman I've met since arriving in Granite Falls."

His heart raced at her approval, and he chastised himself for reacting so strongly to her innocent words. "I'm glad I could be of service, Miss Strong. But I assure you, most people in this new land are honorable, though not always educated in proper deportment. I regret your first experiences with our people were unpleasant."

Her wide eyes lit with curiosity, and he thought they reflected the radiant blue of the sky. "Our people," she repeated. "You sound like Matthew. What is it about this land that makes you feel such kinship with each other?"

Adam's gaze shifted over the greening valley spread before them at the edge of town. During the five years he'd been in Chippewa City, he'd come to love this land and the people settling it. "Perhaps it's the realization that we need each other. One doesn't survive alone here for long. Each person is important, and we all feel the effect if someone doesn't pull his weight."

A rut in the road threw her against his arm, and the faint scent of violets was the same fragrance he remembered smelling through the dust when he had shielded her from the horses. Funny, he hadn't been aware of the scent at the time.

"The road follows the Minnesota River to Chippewa City," Adam said as they left town. He nodded toward the river a hundred yards to their right, where cottonwoods lifted budding limbs.

He watched discreetly as she looked about her at the valley. She sat straight and tall, one gloved hand holding a blue and black striped parasol, the other braced on the seat beside her. "Frankly, I'm surprised to see so many trees, Mr. Conrad. I understood this was prairie land."

He nodded toward the top of the bluff. "It is up there on both sides of the valley. It's only the river valley where there's trees not planted by man. Some of the owners of the timber claims along the river retail their lots out to prairie dwellers for firewood."

Millicent tilted her head back to peer at the top of the bluff, and he wondered what she would think of the prairie. Then he noticed the tight set to her jaw, and he felt a twinge of disappointment; perhaps she was already prepared to dislike it.

The wagon lurched, and Millicent grasped the side of the wagon with her free hand, gasping slightly as she barely kept herself from sliding off the seat. The reins cut into Adam's hands as the horses lunged forward, and he braced his boots against the front of the wagon as the horses dragged them forward out of a narrow hole. He must watch the road more carefully. He'd never forgive himself if his carelessness caused Miss Strong to be hurt.

"Perhaps that is why Matthew feels so needed here," Millicent said. He was surprised that she casually continued the conversation, though her voice was breathless as she smoothed her skirt and adjusted her parasol. "I readily admit I do not understand the attraction the frontier holds for him. After all, there are ill people he can serve back in civilization."

Why should her words cast a pall over his spirit, as if the sun had slipped behind a cloud? Miss Millicent Strong was a beautiful and genteel woman. He would be foolish to expect her to embrace the frontier, yet he realized in astonishment that he hoped she *would* embrace it. "Your brother is the only doctor in this county," he told her. "During the recent typhoid epidemic, he had more than thirty patients, and his route took him over forty miles to care for them. Without Matthew, there would have been no one to look to those patients."

"Typhoid?" The word burst from her lips.

"The epidemic has been over for weeks," he assured her quickly, seeing the fright in her eyes.

"He never told me," she whispered. The color had drained from her cheeks.

"He's fine," he insisted, wishing he could still the fear he heard in her voice. She knew her brother was a doctor; surely she must realize he would be exposed to dangerous diseases. "God watches over Matthew as he tends to the ill."

"Yes," she agreed quietly, but the strange look was back in her eyes. Was it possible she didn't know the Lord? How could that be when Matthew was so strong in his faith? Matthew had never mentioned that she wasn't a Christian. Surely Adam had misread her darting look.

They weren't alone on the road. Open wagons, conestogas, men on horseback, and men, women, and children on foot shared the road, all but a handful headed West. When Millicent changed the subject and asked about them, Adam said, "There's much free land left in Minnesota and further west. The number of people passing through is growing each week, as is the number who stay and settle. A lot different from the way it was last year."

Millicent nodded. "I remember. Matthew wrote of the grasshoppers that destroyed the crops the last few years, and how they scared away new settlers."

Adams jaw tightened, remembering the father that last summer had abandoned Johnny and Pearl, the children Laurina was raising. "Scared away a few of the old settlers, too," he said, and had to clear the huskiness from his throat.

They hadn't gone far before the sound of sledges ringing against steel filled the valley, covering the rumble of the many wagons around them. Adam told her the noise was from the gang working on the Hastings and Dakota Railroad, and pointed to where they were working on the opposite bluff. He explained that beyond this gang were men laying the ties that teamsters unloaded, and beyond them teams and scrapers, and then finally pick and shovel gangs. "It's a boon for the people here. An operation like this employs over a hundred men, many of them locals. The dollar a day the railroad pays sounds good to men who haven't seen a crop harvested for two years."

In a few months Millicent would be able to travel all the way from Illinois to Chippewa City by train. Adam didn't tell her he was glad the railroad stopped in Granite City now. Otherwise they never would have met as they did. He planned to treasure every minute of this unexpected day with her.

A little further along, after they'd ferried across the river, Millicent exclaimed over the purple haze of violets that covered the valley. "They are my favorite flower," she told him, her eyes shining.

He pulled out of the way of the other wagons and jumped

down to pick a handful of the blossoms that hid among the pursch and wild grass. He remembered again the delicate scent of her hair, and he was inordinately pleased when she tucked the flowers into a buttonhole of her jacket-like basque. "Violets are blossoming early this year, due to the open winter," he told her as he climbed back into the wagon.

"Open winter?"

"Not much snow and temperatures mild. It's a blessing for the farmers to be able to get to the fields early. Grass has been green for a month already, and farmers began seeding in the middle of March."

They rode in silence for a few moments, each aware of the other. "How long before we reach Chippewa City?" she asked at last.

"Within the hour." He saw in her eyes the excitement she was trying to bridle. "How long has it been since you last saw Matthew?"

"Three years. I never thought he'd stay in the West this long." She told him then how Matthew had looked out for her when their parents died the year she was fifteen, and how Mrs. Canfield helped her study for her teaching certificate. He'd heard the same story from Matthew, but he didn't say so. He liked to hear her voice.

As she spoke, he searched his mind for the bits and pieces Matthew had told him over the years about Millicent—like the way she stood up to a neighborhood bully who broke a friend's toy when she was ten—and how when she was fifteen she befriended a plain classmate who was teased by the school boys, even going so far as to publicly slap one young man whose remarks were particularly cruel. According to Matthew, she had chosen to support herself by teaching rather than marry any of her numerous suitors. A spitfire, Matthew had called her, his eyes twinkly with laughter and pride. But to Adam, her temper seemed to be reserved for righteous anger. He realized now that he'd come to admire her even before he ever met her.

When he introduced himself, he'd noticed no indication that she recognized his name. He wondered whether Matthew had mentioned him to her, whether she knew he'd been engaged to her brother's fiancee.

They had reached the town by the time she finished her story. As they crossed the bridge over the small falls beside the grist mill, she grew silent. Adam watched as her eyes took in the main street between the five hundred foot treeless bluff and the river.

A shudder ran through her. "I still don't understand how Matthew can choose to live in this place," she said, and with new eyes, Adam looked around the town he'd grown to love.

A dozen log and clapboard buildings straggled along the street, shanty-like and weathered, though all were under ten years old. Buildings, abandoned by settlers fleeing the grasshoppers, stood amidst weeds, their windows boarded. Weeds poked through the street's dust, and footpaths meandered between the spread out buildings. Houses of ill fame mingled with the general store, the newspaper office, the blacksmith shop, the meat market, and hotels. No wonder Millicent thought the town dismal.

At least few drunkards were about, though as the evening approached, more would begin to loiter along the street. Chippewa City had the reputation of the "drinkingest town on the prairie." That was one of the reasons Adam felt so strongly that God had called him here.

"Thomas Jefferson once called our nation's capital a swamp in the wilderness—so perhaps there is hope for Chippewa City, also," he said, wishing he could make her understand how special the town was to him and Matthew.

Her smile chased the frown from her forehead. "A good argument, Mr. Conrad. Perhaps I should reserve judgement for another century?"

"I hope it shall not take us that long to win your praise, Miss Strong."

He stopped in front of the livery. "The horses are too tired after the trip to pull the wagon up the bluff. We'll have to leave it here for the night." Her eyes widened at the road he pointed out. "Matthew's house is on the plateau, about a quarter-mile back from the top of the bluff. Would you like me to rent you a horse?"

She shook her head, looking at the steep road. "I can walk it if you can."

Her gumption pleased him, but he merely nodded and went to speak with the livery owner. He returned a few minutes later with his own mule, Butternut. Taking Millicent's valises and hat boxes from the wagon, he tied them together with a length of rope and slung them over Butternut's back, then helped Millicent from the wagon. He tucked her parasol beneath the rope, and they started toward the bluff.

The road grew steeper as they neared the top, and Adam caught her hand in his as she faltered. She accepted his grasp with a simple trust that filled him with humble joy, even as he said, "I should have insisted on renting you a horse."

"Nonsense," she protested breathlessly. "I've been riding since Illinois. The exercise will do me good."

As they cleared the top of the bluff, the setting sun cast red-gold glory across the land, and Adam's chest ached at the beauty. How gracious of the Lord God to paint the land with light for Miss Strong's first view. Would she like the plateau of which the School Ma'am had spoken so sarcastically?

He kept her hand snug in his own as he watched her absorb the vastness of the land. Her chest rose and fell as she panted from the unusual exertion, and she brushed back a golden lock of hair that had come unpinned. He said nothing, allowing her to take in the wide flat prairie. Only a handful of scattered buildings and a few budding saplings stood between them and the horizon.

"I didn't think it would be like this. Like looking into forever," she whispered, and joy leapt within him at her words.

Ten minutes later they arrived at Matthew's home. They'd just entered the gate to his land when the door opened, and Matthew came out with Laurina, Johnny, and Pearl.

Adam realized with a start that he'd hardly thought of Laurina, not since he'd seen the horses bearing down on Millicent, and he tucked this surprising knowledge away for later review.

With a cry of welcome, Matthew rushed to grab Millicent around the waist and swung her off her feet in a hug of welcome. "Millie! Why didn't you tell me you were coming?" he demanded as he set her down, his hands still at her waist.

Millicent's gloved fingers touched the violets in her buttonhole; they were crushed now by Matthew's welcome, and her gaze flew to Adam's, filled with regret for the bruised blossoms. She adjusted the hat Matthew had almost pushed from her head in his exuberance. "Why didn't you invite me to your wedding?" she retorted, and then added, "And you know I hate to be called Millie."

Matthew laughed, happiness filling his wide face. He grabbed her hand and pulled her toward Laurina as the children ran to greet Adam. Their hugs healed much of the pain in Adam's heart. He felt so good to have Pearl's arms around his neck once more and her innocent kiss on his cheek. As he hugged her close, he watched blonde, fashionable Millicent meet chestnut-haired, simply dressed Laurina.

"I want you to meet the most wonderful woman on the prairie—Laurina Dalen," Matthew announced proudly, throwing an arm around Laurina's shoulders. "Or Boston, as she's known to those of us who love her. Boston, this is my sister, Millie—excuse me—Millicent," he amended with a bow and a grin.

Millicent reached both gloved hands for Laurina's bare ones. "I'm so pleased to meet you, Laurina. I know I shall like you since Matthew loves you so."

Only a slight twinge crossed Adam's chest at her mention of Matthew's love for Laurina, and Adam wondered at the lack of pain.

"Thank you," Laurina was saying in her Boston accent. "How kind of you to come for the wedding. Your presence will be Matthew's favorite wedding gift."

Matthew reached for the valises still thrown over Butternut's back. "How is it you happened across my little sister on her journey, Reverend?"

"Reverend?"

At the soft exclamation, Adam's gaze flew over Pearl's shoulder to Millicent's face. His heart sank at the shock and dismay he saw there. Why should the news of his profession disturb her so?

four

"Reverend?" The word hit Millicent like a blow to the chest. Her eyes sought Adam's, longing for a denial that wasn't there. Instead, he seemed to silently beseech her to accept this part of him. Not certain she could, she hurried to cover her shock. "Reverend. . .Reverend Conrad saved my life." Her gaze never left Adam's face. She was surprised she could get the words out.

Even knowing him such a short time, she wanted this man to respect her. What would Adam think if he knew she didn't believe in God?

And who were these children, she wondered. They looked like angels with their blonde curls and blue eyes. The little girl looked comfortable in Adam's arms. Was it possible the children were his? A pain shot threw her like lightning. The thought that Adam might be married had never occurred to her until now. With a struggle, she forced her attention to Adam's voice.

Blood drained from Matthew's face as Adam told him of the runaway horses, minimizing his own risk. All the adults there, however, knew someone who had been maimed or killed by runaways, and Matthew had to swallow twice before he could thank Adam for saving his sister; his fingers dug deep into Adam's shoulder, saying more than his words.

"Adam, I. . . ." Matthew broke off to look at Laurina, then seemed to gain resolve, and turned back to Adam. "I

39

haven't seen you since Boston. . .since Laurina agreed to marry me. I'll understand if you'd rather not, but it would mean a lot to me if you'd stand up for me at the wedding."

The tension in the air was almost visible, and Millicent didn't understand why. Mr—that is, Rev. Conrad had said he and Matthew were good friends.

Beside her, Laurina was holding her breath. Millicent's gaze darted between Matthew and Adam, finally stopping to search the depths of Adam's dark eyes; she'd already learned that was the only place to read what he was feeling. His face didn't show every emotion as Matthew's did.

She saw his eyes flick to Laurina and back to Matthew before he answered. "I'd be proud to stand up for you, Matthew."

Matthew pounded Adam's shoulder, but seemed at a loss for words, a state in which Millicent had never before seen him. Laurina let out her breath in a soft rush and hurried forward to thank Adam. For the first time since meeting him, Millicent saw a small smile touch Adam's lips.

She hadn't time to wonder over it before Laurina turned to her. "Our day would be complete if you would be my bridesmaid, Millicent."

Millicent had been an attendant for several friends, but never had she been asked to participate the day before the event! Surprise made her hesitate, but only for a moment. "I'd love to be part of Matthew's wedding," she said with a warm smile. "How kind of you to include me."

Matthew slipped an arm around Laurina's waist, and the look he gave her was so full of love that Millicent had to look away.

What was it that made Matthew love this woman so?

Laurina's drab brown dress hung on her, and her equally drab shawl was lifeless next to her gleaming chestnut hair. Simply no one wore a shawl anymore! And Millicent didn't own even a house dress as unfashionable as Laurina's worn brown cotton. Millicent's hands were soft and manicured within their gloves, but Laurina's bare hands were cut and calloused. Why would Matthew choose such a woman when he could have his pick of the sophisticated women in Illinois?

Millicent listened quietly as Matthew and Laurina discussed their wedding plans with Adam. Apparently Adam belonged to a different congregation than Matthew and Laurina, for he assured them he would cut his own service short to make it to the wedding on time. The wedding was to be held immediately after the Sabbath service Matthew and Laurina would attend.

"I'd best be leaving," Adam said. "I'm sure you'd like to visit with your sister, Matthew." He turned to Millicent, and her heart raced as his deep set eyes held her own. "I hope you'll enjoy your visit, Miss Strong."

"I'm sure I shall. Thank you for your kind service to me today."

Adam touched his hat. "It was my pleasure. We shall talk again at the wedding." The intensity in his dark eyes sent a shiver of anticipation through her.

The little girl threw her arms about his neck and planted a damp kiss just above his beard; the boy shook Adam's hand solemnly. Millicent felt a rush of relief when Adam departed without the children. But to whom could they belong?

Knowing she'd see Adam again at the wedding eased her sense of emptiness at his leaving. She didn't try to understand the feelings that overwhelmed her for the sober young man she'd only known a few hours; later, she'd have time to examine them.

She pulled her gaze from Adam's back as he went through the gate and turned to Matthew. "Are you going to introduce me to these delightful children?"

"Forgot you didn't know them," Matthew said with his usual easy grin. He rested a hand on the shoulder of the boy leaning against his leg. "This is Johnny, who's almost seven." He nodded toward the little girl who was standing in front of Millicent, looking up at her curiously. "And that's Pearl, who will be three in another week."

Millicent smiled at the children. With their blonde curls and blue eyes, they looked enough like Matthew to be his own. She pushed the thought from her mind. Likely Laurina was a widow, and the children were from her first marriage. The thought of Matthew being a second husband felt strange. "How do you do, Johnny and Pearl?"

"This is your Aunt Millie, kids."

"Really, Matthew, these children are old enough to say Aunt Millicent, aren't you?"

Johnny merely nodded and leaned harder against Matthew. Pearl's eyes sparkled. "A'n' Mill'cen'," she declared with a self-satisfied nod, and Millicent's heart tumbled to her.

Millicent turned to Laurina. "Tell me, what is your wedding gown like?"

She was dismayed to see Laurina's face flush and her gaze drop to the ground. "I haven't a special gown. We haven't had much time to plan, you see."

Matthew's arm circled Laurina's shoulders. "We've only been engaged two weeks. Laurina's father is a pastor, and he's been called to another church in the Black Hills. We wanted him to perform the ceremony before he left following Easter services next week—so we won't have the grand wedding Laurina deserves."

Millicent tried to hide her surprise. A two week engagement! And Laurina's father a pastor, like Adam. This is Matthew, she reminded herself. You can trust his decisions. She put all the warmth she could into her voice. "I'm sure the service will be lovely. And how nice your father can perform the ceremony, Laurina."

A yipping sound came from the house, and the scratching of claws on wood. "That's Mr. Wiggly," Johnny announced, darting toward the building with Pearl right behind him. A black puppy tumbled out as soon as they opened the door, and the children fell on him in a fit of giggles. Millicent was thankful for the interruption that broke the tension between the adults.

"Laurina, you're only a couple inches shorter than me, and we're almost the same size. I have a new gown with me I'd love you to wear for the wedding."

"Oh, I couldn't," Laurina said firmly, lifting her chin.

"I realize I might be a bit presumptuous," Millicent hurried on, "but we are going to be sisters, and who can give a new dress to a woman if not her sister? Besides, it's rose, which is 'just the color for weddings this year,' according to the magazines." She laid a hand on Laurina's arm and smiled into her brown eyes. "Please," she urged gently.

Laurina seemed to struggle for a moment with her pride. "Thank you, Millicent," she said at last. "If it fits, I'll enjoy wearing it all the more because it belongs to Matthew's sister. But I shall only agree to borrow it."

"Wonderful! Matthew, if you'll carry my valises into the house, Laurina can try the dress on immediately."

Her smile faded as she entered the small clapboard house. The door opened directly into a large, L-shaped room, a combination kitchen, office, and examining room. The walls were whitewashed, bare of the wallpaper popular back East. A bench stood along the wall beside the door, and a cupboard filled with jars of herbs and medicines was against another wall. On the bare wooden table in the middle of the room was a marble mortar and pestle. A curtain was drawn across the back of the room, hiding an examination area. In front of the curtain sat an oak rocker with a worn braided pad. A rolltop desk with a kerosene lamp on top stood against the room's shorter wall, beside a ladder-like set of stairs leading to the second floor. A small kitchen filled the short leg of the "L," with a wooden counter, a handmade cupboard with flowers carved across the top, and a worn table with yet another crude bench beside it. There was barely room to walk, and Millicent wondered how Laurina would ever be able to cook in such a tiny space. The floor had no rugs and the windows no curtains, though wooden shutters did border the windows.

Millicent bit back the questions on her tongue and urged Matthew and the children outside. "It isn't proper for a man to see his bride in her wedding finery before the ceremony," she reminded Matthew.

Matthew leaned against the door jamb with his hands in his pockets and gazed at Laurina. "I won't be seeing anything but Boston's face tomorrow, anyway."

Millicent could almost see the band of love that passed between the two of them. Would a man ever love her this much? A twinge she'd never felt before pulled at her heart. She had to force herself to speak. "Get out of here, Matthew, and let us get on with it. Do I have to remind you how little time we have before the ceremony tomorrow?"

He chuckled as he herded the children out the door, Mr. Wiggly living up to his name as he squirmed in Johnny's arms.

"My word, but that man loves you!" Millicent exclaimed as she bent over her valise.

Color spread across Laurina's face as she said softly, "It's so kind of you to lend me the gown. I haven't anything else special to wear tomorrow."

Millicent carefully removed the rose silk moire from her valise. The gown rustled as she shook the folds from it. "No veil?"

Laurina shook her head. "Times have been hard here, you see, and there hasn't been money for unnecessary things."

Unnecessary! The beautiful trimming for the most special day of a woman's life unnecessary? "And what will you do for flowers?"

Laurina pointed to Millicent's crushed violets. "I'd rather have the wild flowers of the prairie than any others."

Millicent felt a smile tug at her lips. She could understand Laurina's love for the wild flowers. "You'd best step behind this curtain and try on the dress."

Later Laurina and the children left for Laurina's parents' cabin, half a mile away on the plateau, and Matthew and Millicent went back into the house together. "Tell me everything you've been doing since you last wrote, Millie."

"Oh, no," she insisted, clutching his hand and tugging him to the oak swivel chair beside the desk. "You're the one who is going to talk. I have several questions for you."

He turned the chair to face the room before dropping into it, grinning as he stretched his long legs. "Such as?"

Millicent lowered herself primly to the edge of the rocking chair. "Such as, has Laurina been married before?"

He shook his head. "No."

She took a deep breath. "Then, are Johnny and Pearl her brother and sister?"

The grin left his face. "No, they aren't related to her."

"But—"

"When their mother died last July, their father abandoned them. Laurina took them in and has raised them as her own."

A frown creased Millicent's forehead. "Don't they have relatives? I suppose there's no orphanage out here yet, but surely there must be one in Minneapolis or St. Paul."

"Laurina didn't want the children raised in an orphanage." Matthew pulled himself erect in the chair. "The Children's Home in St. Paul is full to overflowing, three to a bed and even the hallways full. Not too many people are adopting during these hard years." He pressed his lips together in a firm line. "Sometimes I think Laurina supported them on a wish and a prayer. She got a little money from the poor fund here, and it hurt her pride like everything to take it. She wrote a few articles for a newspaper back in Boston, and that brought in a bit of money. Her father and Adam brought her wild meat whenever they could." He shook his head. "Just a wish and a prayer."

Adam brought Laurina and the children wild meat? Millicent didn't dare ask why; she didn't want Matthew to suspect her feelings for the Reverend were already far beyond what a decent woman should feel for a man she'd known such a short time.

"Boston and I are going to raise the children together, Millie." His voice dared her to challenge his statement.

Instead, she said softly, "If it weren't for you and Mrs. Canfield, I might have been sent to an orphanage when Mother and Father died—or been sent out unprepared to make my own way in the world. I'm beginning to understand why you called Laurina 'the most wonderful woman on the prairie'."

"Thanks, Millie." He coughed to cover the huskiness in his voice.

"But I do think it's unacceptable to bring a woman and two children into this house. However do you expect a family to live in a place that is nothing more than an overgrown office?"

He raised blonde eyebrows. "What do you mean?"

She stood and threw out her arms. "What do I mean? Look about you, Matthew! There's not a sitting room in this building, nor one upholstered piece of furniture. Laurina will barely be able to turn around in the kitchen, and as for the bedchambers, well, it might be indelicate for me to ask, but where do you plan for the children to sleep?"

Matthew's face burned. "I thought they could sleep on straw ticks on the floor down here."

"How long do you expect that to last?" She propped dainty fists on her hips.

"Until we can afford to build on the house."

"And when will that be, Matthew?"

He shrugged uncomfortably. "I don't know, Millie. Times have been hard here."

"So I've heard."

"It's hard to bring fancy furniture and planed lumber across the prairie in wagons, and that's all we've got until the railroad reaches here."

"You'd best begin planning for a larger home as soon as the tracks reach town, Matthew." She looked around her. "By the way, where am I going to sleep tonight?"

His grin was back. "*I'll* sleep on a straw tick down here, and you can have my bed upstairs."

"I guess I'd better see about checking into a hotel tomorrow," she said thoughtfully. "I assume this town does have a hotel?"

He nodded. "Two of them: Valley House and the Chippewa City House. I wouldn't allow you to stay in either place."

"I assure you I can afford it, Matthew."

He frowned. "That isn't my concern. The hotels are no place for an unchaperoned lady. They see their share of drunkards and—uh—other undesirables. Besides, I've stayed at the Chippewa City House myself when I first came here. There's a store on the first story, and the floor is good old mother earth. All the guests sleep together in an open loft above the store. I'm sure Boston's folks will let you stay with them, though. Johnny and Pearl will be staying there too for a couple of days."

"But I couldn't stay with strangers!"

"You should have thought of that before dropping in unannounced." He softened the statement with a grin as he stood up and pulled her to her feet. "But I'm glad to see you." He hugged her, a quick, tight grasp, and turned toward the kitchen area. "Guess I should see what I have in the way of food. You must be hungry after your trip."

"Famished! But there are other things to consider first."

"Like what?"

"Like, do you have a mercantile here? And is it open?"

"Yes to the first, no to the second. In case you haven't noticed, it's lamplighting time. Mercantile will be closed."

"Well, it's a small town. I suppose you know the owner."

"Yes." He crossed his arms and waited.

"You'll have to convince him to open up again."

"Why?"

"Because your bride doesn't have a veil. I intend to buy a length of lace and make her one."

"But we're getting married *tomorrow*!"

"Yes, so the sooner you get the man to open the mercantile, the better."

Matthew sat up late with her as she stitched the veil to a large comb. They caught up on each other's lives as she worked by lamplight, the odors of coffee and wood smoke filling the small house.

When Matthew mentioned Adam, Millicent pretended to study her stitches and asked, "Do you know Rev. Conrad well, Matthew?"

"He's my closest friend."

She lowered the lace to her lap and tried to look into his eyes, but the lamp that lit her sewing cast shadows across his face. "If you are such good friends, Matthew, why did you wait till now to ask him to stand up for you?"

Even in the dim light, she could see his mouth tighten. The clock on his desk ticked away sixty seconds, then thirty more. She decided he wasn't going to answer and went back to her stitches, hoping Matthew wouldn't notice the tremor of her hands as she asked another, more important, question. "Is the reverend married?"

"Adam? No." He propped his elbows on the arms of the desk chair and ran his fingers through his hair, the lamplight glinting on the golden strands. "I may as well tell you. If I don't, someone else will."

A quiver of apprehension ran through her. What could he tell her about Adam that would be so dreadful?

"Until two weeks ago, Boston was engaged to marry Adam. He broke it off because he knew I loved her."

Millicent felt as though her heart had been dropped over the edge of the bluff. Adam in love with Laurina! That explained the tension she'd felt between him and Matthew earlier. But why should she care? She was only going to be here a few days; she and Reverend Adam Conrad would never have anything but the briefest of friendships. Besides, he was a minister, and she could certainly never love a minister.

Yet her fingers grew cold as she completed the wedding veil for the woman Adam loved.

five

I can't believe Matthew is being married in a one room schoolhouse, Millicent thought, looking around at the backless unpainted benches and the walls' narrow white boards. Matthew had explained that with the hard years, the townspeople couldn't afford to build churches yet, but she wished for someplace nicer for her brother's wedding.

The Sunday worship service was over, and the congregation was waiting outside while Hannah, Laurina's tall, wiry step-mother, piled fragrant wild flowers on the wide window ledges and made bouquets of violets and new fern for Laurina and Millicent to wear. The laughter and voices of chattering adults and playing children filtered through the uncurtained windows, adding to the undercurrent of excitement in the quiet room.

Laurina picked up the ivory backed mirror from the bench beside them and examined her hair, patting the chestnut waves. She pushed a tortoiseshell pin deep below a curl and scowled into the looking glass. "Does my hair look all right, Millicent? I haven't curled it in so long; it feels as though it will fall down if I take a step."

"It won't fall and it looks lovely. As fashionable as any drawing in *Harpers Bazaar*."

"Thanks to you and your curling tong."

"Your hair is beautiful with the rose dress." It was true. The ruching at the throat framed Laurina's slender face

51

and made a soft background for the long twist of hair that touched her shoulders, dangling from combs high at the back of her head.

The dress was the prettiest Millicent had ever owned. The tightly fit bodice came to a V in front, lace filling the ruching-edged triangle from neck to waist, while bows of rose satin caught the draping at the sides of the modest bustle. Tiny matching bows peeked from the lace and ruching at the wrists, and three deep rows of lace fell above the fine pleats of the hem. The brocade fabric caught the light of the prairie morning and tossed its color across Laurina's cheeks, as though trying to compete with the glow in her eyes.

A twinge of regret cut through Millicent. The rose silk set off her own complexion and figure better than any of her other gowns, and she would have like to have worn it when Adam saw her today—that is, Reverend Conrad.

She pushed the selfish thought from her mind. No sacrifice was too great to make for Matthew's wedding. Besides, the deep purple gown and matching hat she was wearing instead hardly made her look like a charwoman, though it was much simpler than the rose. The lace edging the neck and wrists was narrow and dainty, with one small bow at the base of the neck.

The bride caught Millicent's fingers in a tight squeeze. "It must be difficult watching your brother marry a woman you don't even know. You've been simply wonderful, Millicent, lending me this exquisite gown and helping with my hair, and acting as though it's perfectly normal for two people to marry after a two week engagement. But I want you to know that Matthew and I have known each

other for almost two years and—oh, Millicent, I do love
him so!"

Impulsively, Millicent pressed her cheek to Laurina's.
"I could never ask for more for my brother." She cleared
her throat. "Now, let's look at you." She tipped her head
to one side, touched an index finger to her chin, and pursed
her lips.

Laurina's hands flew to her hair. She examined the
draping across her narrow skirt anxiously. "What is it? Is
something wrong?"

Millicent kept her face straight. "Something is missing.
Oh, I know!" She pulled her valise from beneath one of
the benches and carefully removed the veil. As she gently
unrolled the veil and surrounded the bride in a mist of lace,
Laurina's tear-brimmed eyes rewarded her late night
efforts.

Voices from the crowd outside were suddenly loud as
Hannah opened the door in answer to a knock. Millicent
looked up from tucking violets in Laurina's hair and veil
and saw Adam. He was framed in the doorway, his black
coat and wide-brimmed hat dark against the sunlight, with
little Pearl hanging tightly to his hand. Millicent's breath
stopped at the sight of him, and her chest ached with
unfamiliar longing as she saw his gaze linger on Laurina.

Pearl darted across the room to Laurina and clapped
both her chubby hands to the chubbier cheeks beneath her
wide blue eyes. "Oooh, look, Adam, Bos'n is *boot*'ful!"

Adam's long legs leapt to catch up to the little girl.
"Very beautiful," he agreed, capturing one of Pearl's
hands again, and the pain in Millicent's chest sharpened.

Laurina took his free hand in both her own, and though

Millicent knelt to whisper to Pearl, she still heard Laurina's soft, "Thank you, Adam. Thank you for everything."

For freeing her to marry Matthew? Millicent's cheeks burned, and she tried to shut her ears.

"Be happy, Laurina. He's a good man."

The huskiness in his voice made the innocent words pulse with intimacy. Millicent was about to take Pearl outside, when Adam cleared his throat and said, "Your bridegroom is growing impatient, Laurina. He sent me to see whether you were ready."

Hannah answered before Laurina could speak. "As soon as the bride is out of sight, you can let the guests in, Reverend." She hurried Laurina toward a borrowed painted screen that hid the corner at the back of the room. From here the bride and bridesmaid would emerge to walk up the short aisle.

Millicent took a step to follow her when Adam's low voice stopped her. "Miss Strong is beautiful too, isn't she, Pearl?"

Pearl frowned in confusion. "Her name is Aun' Mil'cen', Adam."

His lips threatened to curve upward. "You're right, Pearl. Aunt Millicent is beautiful."

"Yes," Pearl agreed with a nod that set her gold curls bouncing.

"Thank you," Millicent murmured. She couldn't look at Adam for fear her expression would show what his words meant to her. Instead, she pulled a violet from the bouquet on the nearby window ledge and tucked it into the tiny blonde braid that framed Pearl's face. The little girl smiled broadly as she reached to touch the blossom.

"Millicent, come join us," Hannah demanded from beside the screen. Millicent flashed a smile at Adam and, with a heart that sang, hurried to join Hannah and Laurina.

Millicent had intended to memorize every moment of the ceremony in order to share it with Mrs. Canfield, but she spent most of the service trying to keep her eyes from finding Adam as they stood on either side of the bride and groom.

She managed to keep her gaze on Pastor Dalen until he came to the words, "for better, for worse; for richer, for poorer; in sickness and in health; as long as you both shall live." She'd never met a man for whom she could make that promise. Until yesterday, until Adam, she thought as her eyes flew to his face. The words whispering in her mind startled her. She was being a silly romantic. He loved Laurina.

He must hurt unbearably hearing Laurina pledge her love to Matthew. Again, Millicent forgot to keep rein on her gaze, and it drifted to Adam's deep set eyes; she found him watching her rather than the bride. Her eyes were trapped by his and her heart dove into her stomach.

She was breathless by the time Adam released her gaze to pull a ring from his pocket and hand it to Matthew. Moments later, they hurried down the aisle and out into the bright prairie sunshine, Adam's hand at her elbow sending shivers of delight along her nerves.

She hugged Matthew, while guests poured from the schoolhouse. Children darted across the school yard's cut grass, shouting to each other, relieved to be free from the constraints of the service. The school yard was packed with people, and Millicent wondered whether the entire town was there.

Everyone who came through the reception line had a story to tell about Matthew. A number of men and women told with tears in their eyes of how he'd saved their families during the recent typhoid epidemic. Matthew seemed to be a part of every life there. Perhaps. . .perhaps Matthew's life wasn't wasted here on the edge of the frontier after all.

Men carried benches outside and into the shade of the clapboard schoolhouse, and women lifted baskets of cups and plates from wagons and buggies. Millicent noticed only a few pieces of good china lined up on the benches. The teacher's desk was also brought outside and covered with white linen, where more wild flowers were arranged around the punch bowl and cake.

"May I bring you some punch, Miss Millicent?" Adam asked as the last guest turned from the reception line.

"That would be lovely, Mr. Conrad. . .I mean, Reverend."

The lips framed by the trim black beard grew pale. "I've been hoping for an opportunity to apologize for not revealing my profession immediately. I realize this must sound absurd, but it simply never crossed my mind to mention that I was a minister."

Millicent caught her hands behind her back and leaned forward slightly. "I thought you were a farmer," she said in a loud whisper. "After all, you weren't wearing a collar, and—" She glanced at his hands and back to his face. "I've never seen a reverend with callouses on his hands. Don't tell me the Bibles are especially rough on the frontier also?"

Surprise flickered across his eyes and turned to amusement. "The Good Book is only rough on the conscience. It's the plough that roughens my hands. I farm a few acres beside my home."

"I see. Well, in the future it would be only fair to warn a person that you are a minister, so that one's spoken thoughts might be censored in your presence."

"I heard no thoughts yesterday that needed censoring."

She hoped it was true. If only she could recall everything she had babbled during the hours they spent together. The scratches he'd received when rescuing her the day before were covered now with dark scabs, and the sight of them reminded her of his strong arms protecting her from the flying hooves. Her purple lace-covered fingers played with the bow at the base of her throat. "I. . .I think I'd like that punch now, Reverend."

"Certainly." He took a step as if to leave, and then stopped. His eyes darkened almost to ebony as he searched her face, and she found it impossible to look away. "I hope you'll not think me forward, but I'd rather you not call me Reverend. I far prefer being thought of as a man to being considered the sword of God, waiting to strike imperfect human beings."

That's the trouble, Millicent thought. I think of him too *much* as a man. "As you wish. After all, Pearl is rather insistent that you refer to me as Aunt Millicent."

Millicent considered the hint of a smile that touched his mouth to be a major accomplishment. A heady sense of self-confidence rushed through her as he moved away. Could she win an honest-to-goodness smile from him before she returned to Illinois?

His place beside her was claimed immediately by a short, red-haired man with laughing eyes who she had met earlier in the receiving line; Charley, his name was, she remembered. He was the only guest who smelled faintly but distinctly of liquor mixed with cigar smoke. Like many of the other men, he was dressed quite casually in a simple, though clean, everyday coat and a plain brown felt hat. Obviously, he was a farmer rather than one of the businessmen; the men of the town were dressed in a manner more familiar to her with black or gray cutaway coats, watch chains shining across matching vests, and derbies or high silk hats tucked beneath their arms.

Charley set his feet wide apart, and crossed his arms over a chest surprisingly large for such a short man. "So, you're Young Doc's little sister from back Illinois-way."

"Yes." *If he doesn't stop nodding his head like a broken toy, I shall forget my upbringing and laugh in his face.* She glanced over his shoulder, which was barely higher than her own, hoping to see Adam. She did see him, but his back was to her, and he was leaning down to listen to a woman with gray hair.

Charley leaned forward, shifted his cigar stub to one side of his mouth, and lifted his bushy red eyebrows. "You ain't spoken for, are you?"

She tried to stop breathing to avoid the foul odor seeping from his body. *If this weren't her brother's wedding, she'd walk away.* "Spoken for?" She managed to speak without taking a breath.

"Spoken for. Hitched."

She looked at him, bewildered.

"You know, hog tied. Engaged, married, whatever."

"Oh!" She let the air escape from her lungs in surprise. "No, no, I'm not, Mr. . . . I'm sorry, I seem to have to forgotten your last name."

"Bender. But never mind—everyone just calls me Charley."

"I see." She took a step backward as casually as possible, trying not seem rude. When he advanced a step closer, she hoped her knees wouldn't buckle from the scent of him.

"So, hows about if we step out whilst you're here?"

"Pardon me?" Surely she hadn't heard correctly.

The bushy eyebrows drew together. "You have a hard time with English, Miss Strong? Never mind, I'm broad minded. With looks like yours, I don't care if you're not smart."

Millicent jerked ramrod straight. For the bridegroom's sister to strike a guest would not be proper, she reminded herself, curling her fingers into fists. "Mr. Bender, I. . . ."

"It's Charley, I told you. So is it okay if I stop over to Young Doc's to see you?"

"Here's your punch, Miss Millicent."

She turned gratefully to take a cup of the cool drink from Adam's hands. Surely she'd be able to act like lady now that a parson was present!

"Don't tell me you're set on courtin' her, too, Reverend. Have to go some to beat me out." Charley rubbed a hand over his cheek and grinned. "Clean shaven, remember?"

"I'm afraid I'll not be in Chippewa City long enough to see any gentlemen, Mr. Bender. I leave on Thursday." She took a sip of the punch, and her arm brushed Adam's. His nearness comforted her after her exposure to Charley, but she hadn't realized she was standing so close to him. Propriety would suggest she discreetly put a more acceptable distance between them, but instead, she wanted to be even nearer to him; she compromised by staying where she was.

Charley's mouth hung open a moment. "Leavin' Thursday?" he cried in dismay.

"It will be Chippewa City's loss, Miss Millicent."

Her eyes met Adam's, and warmth spilled through her in spite of the cool punch she was drinking. He truly wished she were staying; she was sure she could read that message in his brown eyes.

Charley snorted. "It'll be *my* loss, is what it'll be! Why don't you jest stay awhile longer? You've got no husband to get back to." A self-satisfied grin filled his face as nudged the reverend in the ribs with an elbow. "Found that much out already. No husband or fiance."

"I may not have a husband, but I do have a school waiting for my return. I'm a teacher, Mr. Bender."

"A school teacher, with the trouble you have talkin' English? Imagine that."

"Excuse me?" Adam's straight black brows met.

Millicent couldn't keep back a small laugh at his confusion, though she didn't bother to explain Charley's remark. "Did you enjoy the wedding, Mr. Bender?"

He shrugged his thick shoulders. "A weddin's a weddin'. It got 'em hitched, and that's the main thing."

"Yes, quite," she murmured. Millicent noticed Adam look quickly away and wondered whether he was trying not to laugh.

Charley gave a bark of a laugh. "Think Young Doc's

goin' to have a time of it tryin' to tame that new wife of his, don't you, Reverend?"

"I shouldn't think he'd want to tame her. If he doesn't care for her as she is, he shouldn't have married her."

Millicent's gaze darted to Adam's face. Did he mean that—or did his words reveal his wish that Matthew hadn't married Laurina?

"Aw, c'mon, Reverend. The Good Book tells us a wife is supposed to obey her husband." Charley winked at Millicent. "Now ain't that true?"

"It also says in Ephesians Five that a man is to love his wife as Christ loves the church. I expect if a man loved his wife to that extent, he'd be too busy trying to please her to worry about forcing her into submission."

Millicent searched his face. Did the Bible really say that? Did Adam truly believe it? She knew enough about Christianity to know that Christ's love for people was supposed to be a greater love than the world had ever known. What would it be liked to be loved like that?

Hannah suddenly appeared on the other side of Adam. "Before the cake is served, Pastor Dalen would like you to say a special word, since you're the best man and all, Reverend."

Millicent's heart sank. Was she going to have to deal with Charley alone again? But Adam casually took her hand and slipped it through his arm. He nodded to Charley. "Good to talk to you."

"It was nice to meet you, Mr. Bender." Millicent smiled at Charley, trying to hide her relief at leaving his presence. She breathed alcohol-free air once more and leaned a fraction closer to Adam to say in a low voice, "Thank you.

It seems to be your calling to rescue me—first from horses and now from Mr. Bender. I'm not certain which was the more dangerous."

He covered the hand resting on his arm, and the look he gave her sent ripples of delight through her. Perhaps her own feelings were more dangerous even than Mr. Bender.

Pastor Dalen spoke first, and then Millicent. The crowd became very still when Adam's turn came. Millicent could see he clutched the brim of his hat in a white knuckled grip while he spoke.

"I guess it's no secret I think Matthew and Laurina are two of the best people on God's earth," he began, and Millicent ached for him and his public pain. If only Matthew's happiness did not come at such a high cost to Adam! "I truly believe it is God who put them together, and I wish them every happiness. My prayer for them comes from the fifteenth chapter of Romans, verses five and six. And from my heart."

He turned to face the wedding couple, who stood hand-in-hand with Pearl and Johnny standing beside them. Adam's voice didn't falter as he quoted, "'The God of patience and consolation grant you to be likeminded one toward another according to Christ Jesus: that ye may with one mind and one mouth glorify God, even the Father of our Lord Jesus Christ.' Amen." Adam picked up the long knife from the bench and handed it to Matthew. "Now cut the cake, friend. You've kept your guests waiting long enough."

The crowd laughed away their tension and began milling closer to the cake, resuming their conversations.

"Your prayer was beautiful," Millicent said when Adam

turned back to her. "The unity you spoke of would make marriage a magnificent partnership, wouldn't it?" She wondered at the light that sprang to his dark eyes at her words.

She couldn't imagine two people living their lives with one mind toward God, but for a couple to have one mind toward anything, to be living together for something beyond themselves and each other, would be an incredible way to spend life. Was such a marriage possible?

six

Adam could not have said later what he talked about with the wedding guests while they waited for Millicent and Hannah to finish serving the cake. Even while he spoke and listened, his thoughts were filled with Millicent.

He'd been afraid she would be distant after discovering he was a minister. Ever since he'd left her at Matthew's the night before, his heart had been torn by the shock and betrayal he'd seen in her eyes when Matthew called him Reverend.

"The unity you spoke of would make a marriage a magnificent partnership, wouldn't it?" Her words rang in his mind and chased away his doubts about her faith. Surely he had misinterpreted her expression yesterday. She must be a Christian if she felt that way about his prayer.

Millicent certainly had a generous spirit. Matthew had told him she lent Laurina the dress for the wedding; he'd also said all that she had done to give Laurina a veil. When Adam saw Laurina in her wedding finery, he thanked God for Millicent's gift of beauty to Matthew and Laurina on their wedding day. The pain that had flickered across Millicent's face when he said Laurina was beautiful had baffled him, until for the first time since meeting her, he entertained the hope that she might feel even a little of the attraction he felt for her. The joy in Millicent's face when he said she was beautiful sent that hope galloping through his heart like a wild stallion across the prairie.

He'd expected the wedding to be painful, hearing Laurina and Matthew pledge themselves to each other forever, but only his pride was hurt. While they repeated their vows, his eyes sought Millicent's, and what he felt was relief. Yes, relief! Relief that he'd listened to the Lord and broken his engagement to Laurina; that he hadn't married Laurina before meeting Millicent. Laurina would always have a special place in his heart, but she and Matthew belonged together; he was sure of it. And God *did* have someone else for him. Maybe. . .maybe it was Millicent.

Her acceptance of his presence warmed his heart. The way she leaned eagerly toward him when she spoke and smiled into his face so easily, her blue eyes sparkling through her lashes—it was as though she belonged beside him. It was the way he had always imagined it would be with the woman he loved, with the woman who loved him.

Finally, he saw the chance to speak with Millicent alone, and he slipped up behind her as she leaned against the schoolhouse fence, her back to the crowd. "If you need rescuing from anything, I'm free at the moment."

Millicent turned in surprise to laugh up into Adam's eyes, and he caught his hands quickly behind his back before he could draw her into his arms; he'd wanted to hold her from the first moment he saw her standing beside Laurina before the wedding.

"Why, Reverend, are you actually jesting?"

"We agreed you weren't going to call me that anymore."

"Ah, but you haven't called me Aunt Millicent once since the wedding began."

No woman had ever acted so at ease around him, and he

found her playful manner exhilarating. "Well, Aunt Millicent, what have you been thinking about, standing here looking out across the prairie?"

She opened her mouth, then snapped it shut and tried again. "I was. . . ."

"Are you censoring your thoughts for me now, Miss Millicent?" Regret flooded him. He hated to see her spontaneity stifled.

She dropped her gaze to her lap and a rosy glow filled her cheeks. "Yes. Yes, I am."

"Because I'm a minister?"

"No." She lifted sparkling eyes to his once more. "Oh, no, Mr. Conrad. There are simply some things a proper young woman doesn't share with a man."

A man! She thought of him as a man instead of a minister! He stomped out his foolish joy. The woman he married would have to accept him as both a man and a minister.

"Hello, Reverend, Miss Strong."

Adam nodded to the man with the mutton-chop sideburns and thought he'd never in his life so badly wanted to tell another human being to go away. "Art. You've met Miss Strong, I assume?"

"Yes, yes," the man answered, grasping the narrow lapels of his brown-checked coat. "I expect you don't remember me, however, Miss Strong, considering the number of people you've met here today." He leaned back on his heels. "I'm Art Weaver, editor of the *Valley Ventilator*, the local newspaper."

"Yes, I remember."

A pleased smile turned his plump cheeks into round red balls. "I recognize your name as one of our subscribers,

Miss Strong."

"Yes. I wanted to learn more about this area that so fascinates my brother. Matthew is not a good correspondent."

"I'm sure our little paper can't compare with your hometown paper, Miss Strong," Weaver said with false modesty. When she didn't refute him, he continued, "But we're glad for your support. Your interest in our area may serve us both well. You see, I'm also on the school board. One of the other guests mentioned that you're a school ma'am, and I wondered if there were any possibility that you'd be moving to these parts. We sure could use another school ma'am."

"Oh, no!" Millicent bit her bottom lip to catch back her cry. "I didn't mean to be rude. It's just that the idea surprised me so. You see, I'm happy teaching in Illinois, and I've never considered moving."

The editor shook his head and smiled without amusement. "You sound about as excited over our town as the school ma'am who wrote the letter to me last week."

"Yes, I've heard of that letter."

What could there be about the editor's comment to cause her eyes to widen like those of a frightened doe, Adam wondered

The editor stuffed his hands into the pockets of his checked slacks. "It's all I've been hearing about since the paper hit the streets this week. Her letter's so popular I'd hire that school ma'am to write articles—if I knew who she was and where to find her."

"What. . .what was so special about her letter?"

"Hard to explain. Have to read it for yourself. Woman was a might offended by my suggestion that a school ma'am could preempt a section of land here and be married in a matter of months."

"I recall seeing your advertisement for a school teacher."

"Guess the school ma'am who responded has women's suffrage on her little mind." He rocked back on his heels again. "Beats me what a woman could have against getting married and having a man take care of her the rest of her life."

"Have a man take care of her?"

A tingle of excitement ran through Adam at Millicent's sharp tone. He had a feeling he was about to see the "spitfire" Matthew had so often described.

"I should say *she* takes care of the man," Millicent continued. "You've just said she could preempt a section of land. I wonder whose the land would be after the ceremony?"

Adam looked at her curiously. Her words sounded so familiar. Where had he heard them before?

Mr. Weaver chuckled, rose to the toes of his pointed brown shoes, and settled back on his heels again with a bounce. "Well, I don't think the bride and groom today are going to have to worry about that detail. The parson's daughter is not likely to have much in the way of material goods to bring to her marriage."

Millicent's shoulders straightened, and her round chin shot up. Adam realized she was becoming truly angry and tried to head off the storm. "Art. . . ."

But Mr. Weaver kept speaking. "Besides, Miss Strong, a husband promises to support his wife for a lifetime. It hardly seems unfair for her to turn over her assets to him in return. It's common knowledge that men have a better head for business than women. It would be a shame if a woman squandered her father's inheritance through her ignorance, now, wouldn't it?"

Adam saw the set of Millicent's jaw and wondered why Weaver had to be so patronizing. Couldn't he see his attitude wasn't helping him win his argument? "Art. . . ."

But again he wasn't quick enough. This time it was Millicent who ignored him. "A friend of mine inherited a goodly sum from her father two years ago. It took her husband with his wonderful head for business less than three months to run through the entire inheritance." She spoke as if she were hitting each word with a mallet; Adam was glad he was not the one receiving the blows. "When there was none left, her husband took off for parts unknown, leaving her with a young child. The wealthy man's daughter now takes in laundry in order to feed her child. The law, Mr. Weaver, is stupid."

Weaver leaned forward and spoke to her as though she were a child. "The fact of the matter is, Miss Strong, most women don't bring that much wealth to their marriages."

"That depends upon the type of riches for which a man is looking, don't you think, Art?" Adam spoke quickly, but both Weaver and Millicent ignored him. I hope they don't come to blows, he thought, stepping closer to Millicent and slipping a hand beneath her elbow just in case.

"Most men don't bring much wealth to their marriages, either, sir," she said. "And should women be treated as property, simply because so many of them are kept poor by the laws that men have made? Our country fought a war in the last decade to free the slaves. Well, Mr. Weaver, the wife of every man in this country, regardless of her race, remains a slave."

"Not every man treats his wife in the manner of your friend's husband. Most of us are respectable, hard working men who honor our pledge to support our wives."

"Yes, like another friend's husband, who has a position with a bank in Chicago. He supports her very well. But when he becomes intoxicated, which is every few days, he beats her black and blue."

Mr. Weaver had the decency to give in this time. He dropped his whisker-framed chin to his chest and refused to meet her flashing eyes. "Well, you're right, Miss Strong, there should be exceptions to the law for cases of that nature."

"Exceptions? There should be—"

Adam tightened his grip on her elbow. Nearby guests were beginning to listen. "Never heard anyone wear Weaver down to a compromise before, Miss Millicent. You've come about as close to winning this debate as anyone has ever come with our editor."

Her eyes darted around the crowd in surprise as laughter and applause confirmed Adam's comment. He could see her struggle with the desire to continue the argument, but her dignity gained the upper hand. "Mr. Weaver, perhaps we can continue this discussion at another time."

He bowed slightly from his prominent waist. "I'd be honored."

As the crowd went back to their own conversations, Hannah hurried up to them. "Been looking all over for you two. Matthew and Laurina are leaving. They'd like to speak with you first."

The bride and groom were flushed with a joy that spilled out on the guests surrounding them and filled everyone with a festive mood. Millicent hugged them both, and

Adam shook their hands. Then in a flurry of friendly calls and flying rice, they left in Matthew's new buggy for his house half a mile away.

What must it be like to know you are loved, Adam wondered as he watched the buggy disappear. If you could tell a woman of your love with no fear of rejection, knowing she would speak words of love in return, would you feel as wonderfully free as he imagined? Would he ever know?

As he and Millicent helped clean up the school for the next day's classes, his thoughts shifted back to the conversation with Weaver. Where had he heard her comment about the land before? Was it from the letter to the editor? But she had implied that she hadn't even read the letter. Adam had been proud of the way she stood up to Weaver, a strong, confident woman like the woman who wrote the letter—who was also a school teacher. Could they possibly be one and the same? If so, she obviously didn't want anyone to know. He'd honor her secret, if indeed she had a secret.

Pastor Dalen and Hannah departed soon after Matthew and Laurina, taking Johnny and Pearl with them. Adam asked if he might see Millicent to their house, and she agreed with a promptness that made him feel rich.

The prairie grass brushed at Millicent's gown. Her dress was the color of the violets she loved, and Adam noticed that it turned the blue of her eyes to the same shade as the amethysts at her ears.

Just outside the schoolyard, she tripped over a tuft of grass, and he pulled her hand inside his arm to steady her, glad for the excuse. "I should have insisted you ride with the Dalens."

"I'm fine." She turned to meet his eyes, and he thought his heart would beat clear out of his chest for the joy of looking at her. All too soon, she looked away.

"I. . .I apologize if I embarrassed you in front of Mr. Weaver. I can be rather outspoken at times."

"No!" At the surprise in her face, he forced his voice to a more normal level, as he pulled her around to face him, his hands holding her gently but firmly above the elbows. "You didn't embarrass me, Miss Millicent. You could never embarrass me."

He watched her search his face slowly. "I realize there are many pastors today who believe it's sinful to think a woman should not be the property of her husband. I. . .I hope my views were not offensive to you."

"Miss Millicent, judging people is not one of my duties. As a minister of the Gospel of Jesus Christ, I am to share the message of His love and salvation, and serve the people He created. But I didn't hear a great sinner when you debated with Mr. Weaver. I heard a woman who is concerned for hurting people. Your sensitive heart must make Christ glad, because it's people like yourself who take seriously His command to 'love your neighbor as yourself.'"

Her lips parted, and she said in a voice just above a whisper, "You're a most unusual minister, Mr. Conrad."

Her face so close to his tempted him. He released her arms and began walking, sliding her hand through his arm once more. Did her lips taste as sweet as they looked? He clenched his teeth until the muscles in his face hurt. Her soft gasp and sudden tugging of her hand made him realize he'd tightened his grip on her small fingers. He released them and turned to her in consternation. "I'm sorry! Did

I hurt you?"

"No, I'm fine." Her smile was shaky.

His arm felt empty without her touch. He longed to draw her arm back but didn't. They were almost at the Dalens' door.

Everything within him clamored to stay with her, but he simply said, "I hope to see you again before you leave, Miss Millicent."

His eyes drank in her face as she murmured a polite response, and then he turned and started across the plateau to his own cabin. I'll make certain I see her again, he thought.

seven

That evening, after the children and Mr. and Mrs. Dalen were in bed, Millicent slipped outside to stand in the gentle night air and examine her day. The soft symphony of the prairie insects surrounded her as she tipped her head back to the sky.

Never had the night seemed so large to her. With no trees or buildings to hide its width, the sky spread above and around her, full of stars. No wonder Adam and Matthew loved this land. Still, it frightened her somehow.

Adam. His slender face with its trim beard and dark eyes hadn't left her thoughts all evening. She loved his eyes, the way they hid his emotions, yet turned from brown to black when he felt something deeply; the way they sometimes glimmered, hinting at a smile; and most of all, the way his eyes refused to deceive or skirt a painful truth.

Only last night she'd told herself she could never love a minister, and now the man filled her thoughts and heart. She'd been mortified when she'd realized she'd made a spectacle of herself arguing with the newspaper editor. Not that she didn't mean every word she'd said, but she was afraid she'd alienated Adam, and before she left for Illinois she wanted to know him better.

But he hadn't been offended by her views. Instead he thought her sensitive heart pleased Christ. If only he knew she didn't believe in his God! Still, to think anything about her might be pleasing to God had never crossed her mind before.

Silly, though, to allow herself to be so attracted to Adam. She could never be a proper wife for a minister, even if she could stand to live out here without the comforts with which she'd grown up. Stop being a fool! No one could fall in love so quickly.

Besides, he loved Laurina. She could still hear the tension in his voice when he spoke with Laurina before the wedding, and her heart shrank from the memory.

Likely only the emotion of the wedding had attracted her to Adam. Yes, surely that was it. She'd never responded to another man this way. The wedding must be the reason.

Late Tuesday morning, Millicent, Johnny, and Pearl climbed into the Dalens' wagon with Hannah and started for Matthew's house. Pastor Dalen had left just after dawn to help with a room raising for Matthew and Laurina.

Millicent wasn't excited about the plain white sunbonnet Hannah had lent her for the day. She'd have preferred her own small blue hat with feathers that went so well with the blue checked dress she was wearing. The bright sun burning down and the wind whipping across the plateau, however, convinced her of Hannah's wisdom.

Would Adam be at the room raising? She hadn't seen him since the wedding. He'd seemed so attentive that day, but perhaps he'd only been kind to his friend's sister, and hadn't given her another thought. She grinned as they arrived at Matthew's. She'd certainly try to change that, given the opportunity!

Horses and mules were staked out around the fence, and she thought she recognized Butternut among them. She couldn't see the new addition going up, as it was being added to the back of the house, but the noise from the hammering, the men calling to each other, and the children playing set the air dancing. Excitement tingled along Millicent's arms as she climbed down from the wagon.

"Millie!" Matthew was there before her feet touched the ground, wrapping his arms around her in a bear hug that took her breath.

"My goodness, Matthew, with you about a woman doesn't need a corset. And my name is Millicent."

With a laugh, he released her and reached up to help Johnny and Pearl from the wagon bed. "Will Laurina be glad to see you two youngsters! She's done nothing but talk of how she's missed you."

Johnny's face flushed with pleasure at his words, and Millicent's heart went out to the boy. "Come on, Pearl, let's go see Boston." He grabbed his sister's hand, and they ran as fast as her chubby legs would go. She squealed and called, "Bos'n! Bos'n!" Hannah followed along with her hands full of pies. "Might help us carry things, Matthew. Your sister and I have been baking for this shindig since the prairie chickens started booming this morning."

Matthew reached into the wagon bed and pulled out four loaves of towel-wrapped bread. "Hold out your arms, Millie."

"You look wonderfully happy, Matthew," she said, her arms full of yeasty fresh loaves.

He pulled two pies from the wagon and grinned down at her. "I am. You should try this marriage stuff, Millie. When are you going to give in to one those boys you've been seeing back in Illinois?"

She widened her eyes in innocent surprise. "Why, Matthew, I've no intention of marrying a boy. I'm waiting for an honest-to-goodness man."

"Just so he's the best, Millie. I wouldn't want anything less for you."

Tears rushed to her eyes at his husky words. "Why didn't you tell me you were adding another room when I pestered you the other night, Matthew?"

"Wasn't planning one. It's a surprise from our friends," was his rough-voiced reply.

He led the way toward the group of women beside the house, and they set the bread and pies on a makeshift table, a wide plank across two barrels. Quilts brightened the new prairie grass, where people were lunching picnic-style. Half a dozen women were preparing food, three teenage girls helping.

Johnny yanked on Matthew's forearm. "What took you so long? Goin' to help me carry in our clothes and Miss Millicent's bags, Young Doc? Boston said to bring them in and put them away, and that you'd know where they go. Can I help the men with the buildin', Young Doc?"

"Expect there's a job that's just waiting for you, Johnny. Talk to you later, Millie." Matthew bumped the back of his knuckles against Johnny's shoulder. "Race you to the wagon."

Millicent smiled as she watched them. Matthew was going to make a wonderful father.

"Welcome, Millicent." She turned to find Laurina beside her, looking as radiant as the day she was married. "Come meet our friends."

Because she was used to remembering the names of a roomful of students, she surprised them by recalling all their names after only one introduction. She wondered, however, if she'd remember them if she saw them again. They were all wearing sunbonnets that hid their hair and cast shadows over their faces. Millicent joined Stina, a heavy set woman in a plain brown dress. Together they peeled potatoes, which were soft after being stored over the winter. Millicent liked Stina's friendly smile, and was pleased to find her as kindly as her face.

Millicent placed herself where she could watch the men as she pared potatoes and asked Stina to point out her husband. Stina pointed her knife toward the largest man in the group. "That's my Olaf. The young one beside him is our eldest son, Thorburn."

The "young one" had broad shoulders and muscled forearms. Millicent thought he must be at least sixteen.

A dozen men worked on the addition, sawing, hammering, or holding wood for the other workers. She immediately picked out Adam's back, his gray collarless shirt wet with sweat, the black hair in damp ringlets against his neck. Her pulse raced at his nearness.

Johnny had carried a bucket of water to the work area, and was importantly carrying dippers of water to each of the men. Millicent watched Adam turn around to accept the drink; he drained the dipper and caught sight of her just as he lowered it from his lips. The dipper stopped in mid-air as their gazes locked. She offered him a slight smile. What did he think of her in the bonnet? He nodded, as solemn as always, and went back to work.

Two fires burned in the yard. Over one was hung a kettle on which water was heating for the potatoes, and a hog was roasting on the other. The aroma from the food blended with the smell of new lumber and spring prairie grass.

The meal took a little over an hour to prepare. When it was ready, the men washed up in cold water, splashing it over their heads and necks. Roast pork, a kettle of mashed potatoes, a bowl of gravy, plates of sliced bread, fresh butter from Stina's farm, and bowls of beans crowded the table. After filling their plates, families joined each other on the quilts, while the unmarried men shared a quilt of their own. At Matthew's insistence, Millicent joined him and his new family, but her eyes strayed to Adam. As much as she enjoyed being with Matthew again, she wished Adam had asked her to sit with him.

Stina's son Thorburn looked longingly toward Ellie Brandt, a girl about his own age who wore her hair in a long brown braid. Millicent decided she wasn't the only one wishing she had someone else's company.

The men had hearty appetites after the morning of hard work, and before long all the food was gone. Matthew stood, drawing Laurina up beside him with an arm around her waist. He gave a loud whistle, and when everyone had quieted, said, "Boston and I want to thank each of you here today for the gift of your time and effort. Guess you know this came as a surprise to us—but we sure can use the extra room. We'd especially like to thank Adam for the lumber and for talking all of you into leaving your fields for a day. It's a sacrifice for you at this time of year, and Boston and I can't tell you how much it means to us." He dug his hands into the pockets of his denim pants. "Guess Chippewa City just grows people especially good. Don't want to get all sentimental on you, so help yourselves to some of this pie my sister made, before I embarrass myself."

Everyone started talking at once as they took Matthew up on his invitation to dessert. Millicent turned to Laurina.

"Adam gave this lumber?"

Laurina nodded. "It was awfully generous of him, wasn't it? But then, Adam is like that. I'm sure he couldn't afford it any better than Matthew and me right now, but we could hardly say no when he arrived this morning right after sunup with all these men ready to begin building."

"Of course not," Millicent mumbled as they followed the others to the table.

She and Laurina were the last to serve themselves. She poured fresh cream over a piece of pie, then looked up to find Adam standing across the table from her. Her heart suddenly pounded.

"Your pie is delicious, Miss Millicent. I thought you might not care for cooking since you are such a staunch supporter of women's rights."

Did she dare hope his statement meant he had been thinking of her since she'd last seen him? "I also believe in eating well, Mr. Conrad." She motioned toward the addition, which had now been completely framed. "Is this the lumber we brought from Granite Falls?"

"Most of it."

"You're very good at keeping secrets. You didn't even hint that it was a wedding gift for Matthew and Laurina."

"It wasn't." Consternation filled his face, and the cheeks over his beard reddened. "I didn't intend to say that. The lumber was originally meant for my house, but Matthew and Laurina are more in need of it." He set his empty plate down on the table and pulled a hand across his beard, embarrassment filling his dark eyes. "It sounds so . . .so pompous to put into words."

"No," she said softly. "It sounds kind." Yet she wondered if he'd been planning to improve his own home in anticipation of his marriage to Laurina, and her heart smarted. What must it be like to be loved by such a man?

The afternoon flew by for Millicent as she helped the other women clean up the dinner dishes, then visited with them until it was time to begin dinner.

Once Millicent noticed Adam teaching a eager Johnny to pound nails. The hammer struck Adam's thumb instead. She knew it must throb, but Adam only grit his teeth, poured a dipper of water over his bruised finger, and encouraged Johnny to try again.

Millicent's thought strayed often to Adam during the afternoon. She'd never met such a unique man. First he walked away from the woman he loved so Matthew, his best friend, could marry her. Then he not only gave them lumber he'd planned to use for his own home, but he recruited the neighbors to help in improving the home of the man who married the woman he loved. How could a person give up so much for another? How could one love so much, forgive so much? Did his faith help him to do these things?

By lamplighting time the room was completed. The evening meal was over, the supper dishes done, and everyone began climbing into their wagons or walking across the fields toward their homes.

Millicent thought at first that Adam would leave without speaking to her again, but when he had hitched Butternut to his empty wagon, he came to the door where she waited while Laurina and Matthew said goodbye to other friends. Like the rest of the men, his clothes and hair was still damp with sweat. She saw his gaze touch her hair for a moment and was glad she was no longer wearing the voluminous sunbonnet.

"I have a mid-week service tomorrow night, Miss Millicent. I hoped you might be able to come."

If only she could! "I'd like to, but I leave the following day, and I want to spend time with my brother."

"Of course. I should have realized." He turned his hat around in his hands and seemed to search for some reason to postpone his leave-taking. "I enjoyed meeting you, Miss Millicent. I hope we'll see each other again before you leave."

He'd just placed his hat on his head when Matthew came up and slapped him on the back. "Adam, that was the best wedding gift of them all. We can't thank you enough."

"It was gladly given by all who helped. I'd best be leaving. Johnny and Pearl are about asleep already." He nodded at the abnormally quiet children sitting on the ground a few feet away, Pearl leaning against Johnny with her thumb in her mouth.

"Well, guess we'll see you at church tomorrow night then, Adam. Pastor Dalen's not holding a service, so thought we'd go to yours."

Adam's eyes darted to Millicent's, and the hope in them made her bubbly inside. "May I join you at the service, Matthew?" she asked, her gaze still holding Adam's.

"Sure would hate to leave you home when you travelled all the way from Illinois to be here, Millie."

Adam touched a hand to the brim of his hat. "Then I'll be seeing all of you tomorrow night."

When the children were cleaned up and ready for bed, the adults gathered for devotions in the room they called the parlor. Millicent wasn't accustomed to devotions being part of her day, and she found the experience uncomfortable. She'd seen Mrs. Canfield read the Bible often, but they had never read it together or prayed together, other than to say grace at meals.

Matthew began the devotions by reading a selection from the Bible. He opened the large black book, looked down at Johnny's curls resting against his chest, and winked at Laurina. "Think we'd better keep it short tonight." Millicent was quite pleased with herself when she recognized his choice as Psalm 23.

But she wasn't prepared to hear herself mentioned when Adam prayed. After thanking God for the new addition and their friends, he continued, "and thank Thee, Father, for bringing Millie to share this special time in our lives. Bless her for the love she's shown us. Make this trip a blessing to her and fulfill Thy purpose in her life. Keep us all in Thy arms as we slumber this night. In Jesus Name, amen."

Millicent hoped she didn't look as embarrassed as she felt when she lifted her head, but she needn't have been concerned. Matthew and Laurina were preoccupied with getting the children to bed. After their long day, even the prospect of sleeping in the new room couldn't excite them.

Matthew had place a straw tick on the "parlor" floor for Millicent, and she lay on it after everyone else was in bed, pondering Matthew's prayer. What had he meant when he asked God to fulfill His purpose in her life?

eight

The services the following night were held in the school-house. Matthew explained to Millicent that Pastor Dalen's church and Adam's church shared the schoolhouse for services, alternating periods of use. Otherwise, they met in the homes of members of the congregation.

Millicent was surprised to find the small building almost filled. Were people here more religious than back East, she wondered, or did they simply not want to miss one of the few opportunities to socialize?

She'd never been so eager to attend a religious service. Adam fascinated her. She wanted to know what he would have to say about his God.

She watched his eyes search the people until he caught sight of her sitting with Matthew's family. His search stopped with her face, his sober expression softening. She smiled, a smile small enough no one could consider it improper, though her heart hammered at the sight of him.

The service was informal compared to the proper, solemn services to which she was accustomed back home. No piano or organ accompanied the congregation, but the people sang the opening hymn for all they were worth:

> Joyful, joyful, we adore Thee,
> God of glory, Lord of love,
> Hearts unfold like flowers before Thee,
> Opening to the sun above. . . .

Millicent hung on every word of Adam's sermon, trying

to discover more about this man she'd known such a short time. "Like the flowers open to the sun, God has created us to reach for Him," Adam began. "As we prepare for Easter next Sunday, perhaps we should examine ourselves to see whether we've truly opened our hearts to Christ.

"I'm sure I needn't remind anyone in this room that the last years have been extremely difficult for the people of this area. A year ago this month, Governor Pillsbury proclaimed a day of fasting and prayer for relief from the grasshoppers. The 'hoppers destroyed crops so completely that many people questioned whether they were seeing a repeat of the locust plague the Lord visited on Pharaoh's people during the time of Moses. Many here cried out to God during the grasshopper years, and made promises as to what they would do if He spared our area from destruction. Among those promises were promises to build churches, and many of you have spoken to me of your hope that this will be possible within the next few months.

"I have no doubt that God is glad for the good intentions indicated by those promises. But have we truly repented and relied on God's grace, or have we tried to barter with Him? My friends, we cannot get to heaven by building churches, or by performing other good deeds, for we can never be as good as God."

Millicent leaned forward, unaware of the frown beneath her short, curly fringe. She'd never heard such a thing! How else could one get to heaven if not by being good?

"Good deeds certainly have an important place in the life of a Christian," Adam continued, "but they are the result of believing in Christ, and not the way by which we reach God. The Bible says in Romans 10:9 that 'if thou shalt confess with thy mouth the Lord Jesus, and shalt believe in thine heart that God hath raised him from the dead, thou shalt be saved.'

"Christ kept the law of God perfectly as none of us are able to do, as no man has ever been able to do. He paid the price for our sins by allowing Himself to be crucified. But He was stronger than death and rose to life again. Because He paid the cost of our imperfect lives, we can have salvation by simply believing in Him, and telling God we have decided to take His offer of salvation.

"It's an offer available to everyone in this room. If anyone would like to accept His offer tonight, you may come to the front as we sing the final hymn, 'Amazing Grace,' and I will pray with you."

Millicent knew the words to the familiar hymn, and she stood and sang with the others. Half a dozen people went forward and knelt at the front of the room, and Millicent was tempted to join them. If Adam's God could make it possible to love people the way Adam, Matthew, and Laurina did, she wanted to know Him. But the decision was too important to make without examining it further.

After Adam gave the benediction, the congregation filed out of the building, talking quietly among themselves so as not to disturb those who remained behind. Millicent's gaze lingered on Adam's back, disappointed he was occupied with those who had gone forward. With a sigh, she turned to go.

A hand touched her arm as she reached the door, and her heart lightened when she found Adam beside her, asking if he might accompany her to Matthew's house when he was free.

Forty-five minutes later the church cleared and he joined her. He carried a lantern to guide them, his Bible under his arm. She and Adam walked silently. The only sight they could see in the starless night was half a dozen lit windows spread over the miles of flat land.

The silence began to grow uncomfortable to Millicent. She knew Adam was a quiet man, but she wished tonight, perhaps their last opportunity to be together, he would want to take advantage of every moment.

She was the one who finally broke the silence. "I'm glad I had the opportunity to hear you speak, Mr. Conrad. I've been curious about your religious beliefs."

"My beliefs? Why?"

Here in the dark where the small space between them pulsed with the intensity of her emotions for him, his faith seemed a safe topic. "Because you forgive so completely and love so well. Because...." Did she dare tell him? Yes; in the darkness, they could barely see each other's faces, and besides, she wasn't likely to ever see him again. "Matthew told me you and Laurina planned to marry. I ...I wasn't going to say anything, but I couldn't help but be impressed with the way you forgave her and Matthew, and by your gift to them."

"It's easy to give to those you love, Miss Millicent."

Her heart contracted. He did still love Laurina! Of course he did. Had she really thought he could forget her so quickly? "Perhaps it's easy for you, Mr. Conrad," she forced herself to say. "But for most of us, it would be difficult under those circumstances."

She heard him clear his throat. "Miss Millicent, Christ can help anyone to truly love and forgive."

"That was why I wanted to hear your sermon tonight— to discover if it was your faith that made you...different." She'd wanted to say wonderful, but even in the darkness she hadn't the courage.

"My faith is part and parcel of who I am, Miss Millicent. The Bible tells us God is love. If there is anything at all good or loving about me, it comes from my faith in Christ."

Why did his voice sound so sad? "I've always heard that Christians were to be like Christ, but I've seen little evidence of it, until now."

"Do you want to be like Christ, Miss Millicent?"

She pulled idly at one of her gloves. "I'm not sure. I thought I did, but I believe the challenge is beyond my ability."

"It is beyond all of us. However, once we've accepted Christ's salvation, we can grow a little more like Him each day, if we commit our lives to following Him. It's part of His plan."

"Is it true what you said tonight? That God doesn't expect us to become acceptable to Him by being good? That the only way we can know God is to tell Him we're sorry for being imperfect and thank Him for what Jesus Christ did for us?"

"Yes, Miss Millicent. It only takes a moment."

She could hear in his voice the longing for her to say she was ready to pray now, and she was tempted to do so to please him.

"I would be glad to pray with you if you wish." His voice was as gentle as the night breeze.

She shook her head, then realized he probably couldn't see her. "No. When—that is, if—I decide to accept your God, I must be certain it's the right thing to do."

He didn't respond for a long time, and so greatly did she want his favor, she had to bite her lips to keep from saying she'd changed her mind.

"You're right, Miss Millicent," he said at last. "One shouldn't take such an important step lightly, and if I were thinking more clearly, I wouldn't expect an intelligent woman like yourself to do so."

What did he mean, if he were thinking more clearly? Her question went unasked as he continued, "If you ask God to show you the truth, He will make His word clear to you."

"You mean by reading the Bible? I thought it was too difficult for ordinary people to understand."

"It can seem overwhelming at times. The key is this: the main story throughout the Bible is that God created man for Himself, but we separated ourselves from Him by our sin. His greatest desire is for us to become reunited with Him through faith in His Son, the Lord Jesus Christ. If you keep that in mind, the Bible is easier to understand."

"I've never actually read it before. I don't own a Bible." Why should it embarrass her so to admit that? How many people did she know who read the Bible, or admitted it if they did?

"Miss Millicent, I'd like you to have my Bible."

"But I couldn't! Why, you're a minister. You need your Bible."

"I can get another easily. It would please me to know you were using mine."

A thrill ran along her nerves. She would be pleased too to have something of Adam's to take back to Illinois. "Thank you, Mr. Conrad. It is a generous offer."

His hand rested on the sleeve of the purple gown she'd worn to the wedding. "Would you promise me you'll read it every day?"

Every day? Could she promise such a thing? "It's...it's an awfully large book."

"Yet even one verse a day would fulfill your promise, Miss Millicent."

"Yes, I guess it would at that." Her laugh floated into the night. "I believe I can make that promise after all."

His fingers tightened and his thumb played back and forth on her arm, sending warmth pouring through every inch of her. She felt herself leaning toward him, and his hand slipped to her waist. His breath against her cheek was warm and quick. She lifted her hand to his shoulder, eager to feel his embrace.

She heard him swallow hard before moving away. "You have a tiring day of travel ahead of you tomorrow. I should be leaving so you can get your rest."

Disappointment flowed through her veins as he took her elbow and led her to the house that was a mere silhouette against the night sky. She'd hoped against hope he'd tell her he cared for her. To think she'd be leaving tomorrow and never see him again!

"Here is my Bible, Miss Millicent," he said as they reached the door.

The book was warm from his hold, and she clutched it against her, welcoming something that was so much a part of him.

"Miss Millicent. . . ."

She held her breath, waiting for him to continue, longing for him to draw her into his arms.

"I'm very glad you came to Matthew's wedding, Miss Millicent. I hope you'll return one day."

"I'm glad I came too, Mr. Conrad."

Then his hand cupped the back of her neck, and his beard brushed against her cheek as his lips pressed warmly against her temple.

"Adam——" she cried softly, turning her face toward his kiss.

But his lips didn't touch hers. "God keep you, Millicent." His hoarse voice cracked on the words.

And he was gone, before she could return his caress. Her arms ached for the lost opportunity to hold him. "Goodbye, Adam," she whispered into the night. A tear fell on the worn leather of his gift.

nine

Foolishness, to let yourself touch her like that, Adam raged as he crossed the plateau to his home. His name on her lips had almost been his undoing. He'd wanted to hold her forever, not allow her to go back to Illinois where he couldn't see her or talk to her, where he'd have no chance of preventing her from falling in love with someone else.

As if he could prevent such a thing anyway. He'd spent a good deal of time the last two days in prayer over Millicent, asking God's guidance, asking Him to help him keep a rein on his feelings. His experience with Laurina should have taught him not to run ahead of God's leading. He knew it was too soon to care so much for Millicent.

He groaned. To care for a woman who wasn't a Christian! He should have realized. He'd hoped her generous spirit was evidence of her faith in Christ. What a servant of God she would make with her sensitive heart and strong character!

That was the important thing, of course. Even if he never saw her again—and his heart shrank at the thought— he could stand it easier if he knew she was a Christian and had God walking with her through her life.

When he reached his dark cabin on the edge of the settlement, he dropped to his knees beside his narrow bed and begged the Lord to never give up until He won Millicent's heart for His own.

Adam looked about at the wagons, buggies, and people filling his unfenced yard, and tried to feel as thankful as he knew he should for their presence. The pound party would provide food for him for weeks and relieve the guilt of parishioner who during these hard times hadn't been able to pay his full salary of twenty-three dollars a month. Still, talking pleasantly was difficult when his heart was aching. Millicent had been gone for six weeks now, but she'd never left his thoughts.

He was glad to see the people so happy, though. This spring the grasshoppers that had devastated the crops the past few years were gone, and the railroad promised new life for the community. Already new settlers were taking up the lands left behind by those who moved further West when the 'hoppers came. Optimism was back, and it made generosity possible.

"Made up your mind which basket you're going to bid on, Adam?" Matthew's hand landed on his shoulder in a friendly slap.

Adam looked toward the wagon bed where the owner of the mercantile was holding up a basket draped in blue checkered cloth and tied with a bright red ribbon. Mrs. Moyer, the banker's wife, stood beside the merchant, encouraging the crowd to increase their bids. The blue checked cloth reminded Adam of the dress Millicent wore the day of the room raising, and a streak of pain burned his chest. Would he ever be able to forget her?

"I appreciate the many pounds of food the people have given me, Matthew, but I wish it didn't come with hints that I should be courting one of their daughters."

Matthew's laugh sprang out. "I thought I'd noticed an

unusual number of mothers toting along marrying-age daughters today."

His laughter did nothing to lift the gloom from Adam's shoulders. "You wouldn't find it so funny if you were on the receiving end."

The blue checkered basket went to Stina's son Thorburn, and Ellie Brandt, with a matching checkered bow on her long brown braid, smiled up into the Norwegian's broad face. A basket with a bandanna tied in a bow on the handle was lifted up next.

"Isn't that a creative way to do up a basket, Reverend Conrad?" Mrs. Jacobs, one of his parishioners, hurried up to him breathlessly. Before he could respond, she said, "My daughter Hilda made it up. She's a very good cook, you know." She leaned closer to say, "There's fried chicken in that basket. And raisin cookies you wouldn't believe!"

Matthew had to turn away to hide his laughter from the eager mother, and Adam could have cheerfully kicked him. He pointed toward the wagon. "I do believe Mr. Yates has won your daughter's basket, Mrs. Jacobs. A good man, Mr. Yates."

Mrs. Jacobs threw her shoulders back and set her mouth primly. "Yes," she agreed between clenched teeth and stormed toward her daughter and the young farmer.

Matthew turned back, still chuckling. "Have they all been that obvious?"

"Most of them."

"How long do you think you'll be able to hold out against them?"

Usually Adam enjoyed Matthew's wit, but not today.

"If you're asking if I'm attracted to any of these young women, the answer is no. And none of them are attracted to me, I assure you. I'm just a sober old man to most of them." Not one of them had ever smiled up at him with a quick smile that lit her face like Millicent's, or had the courage to speak what she thought in his presence as Millicent had.

Matthew's grin grew wider. "Their mothers consider you good marriage material."

"Can't imagine why. Certainly not because of my secure income. Why would any mother want her daughter to rely on handouts and pound parties?"

"Guess they figure God isn't going to let a minister's wife starve." He pushed his hat back on his blonde hair and crossed his arms. "If you want these women off your back, maybe you should just get married. That would do the trick."

If only he could! "I can't marry the woman I love, Matthew."

His friend sobered instantly. "I'm sorry, Adam. I forgot you and Boston were engaged."

"I didn't mean—"

Matthew held up a hand. "I've never thanked you for giving her up. We've been married less than two months, and already I can't imagine life without her." He looked down at his dusty boots and kicked at a tuft of prairie grass. "I forget sometimes that you love her too."

"I wasn't referring to Laurina."

Matthew looked up in surprise. "You weren't?"

Adam laughed at his friend's expression, glad to be able to laugh again. He hadn't for a very long time. "As much as I care for and respect your wife, may I remind you there are other women in the world a man could love?"

Matthew looked sheepish. He dug his hands into his back pockets. "Yeah, I guess there are at that. But I haven't noticed you courting any of them. Only woman I've seen you with is Millie." He took a deep breath. "Boston prays every day that God will bring a great love into your life, Adam. She says you deserve the best woman in the world."

Adam could see from the pain in Matthew's face how much it cost him to reveal Laurina's prayer. "Well, it would seem her prayers are answered. Only, as I said, I can't marry the woman."

"If I'm butting in where I shouldn't, just say the word— but why can't you marry her?"

"Because she isn't a Christian. And we both know what the Bible says about Christians marrying nonChristians."

Matthew nodded. "'Be ye not unequally yoked together with unbelievers,'" he quoted from Second Corinthians Six. "I'll be praying for you, Adam, that this woman becomes a follower of Christ." He grinned. "Whoever this mystery woman is." His smile faded. "It isn't. . .not Millie?"

Adam nodded and watched sorrow fill his friend's eyes. "Are you sure she's not a Christian, Adam?"

"Yes, we discussed it."

"We always went to church together. I just assumed—"

Charley's drunken voice interrupted them. "Yahoo! That's the basket for me!" He urged his big bay through the crowd to stop beside the merchant and Mrs. Moyer. Charley grabbed for a basket draped in yellow, but the merchant lifted it out of his reach.

"Money first, Charley."

Charley gave a wobbly grin and removed his feet from the stirrups. "Got to see if it's worth it." Before anyone realized his intention, he tried to stand up on his saddle. Adam felt his blood run cold at the sight. The crowd held their breath as Charley wobbled.

"Didn't think I could do it, huh?" Charley lunged unsteadily for the basket, lost his footing, and fell between the wagon wheel and his horse. His horse leapt aside with a frightened whinny.

Matthew and Adam darted forward. The crowd opened for them, then closed again around the drunken man who now lay silent. The prairie wind and the nervous snorts of Charley's horse were the only sounds in the crowded yard as Matthew kneeled beside Charley.

He was unconscious, a gash on his forehead bleeding profusely. Matthew tried to stop the flow by applying pressure to the wound.

"You can put him in my bed if you want, Matthew."

"Thanks, Adam. Olaf, Thorburn, you two have good strong muscles. Help the Reverend and me move him."

Under Matthew's guidance, they moved him carefully, laying him on the rough blanket that covered Adam's bed. Laurina hurried into the room with a bowl of cold water and a towel she'd found in Adam's kitchen.

"Looks like the horse kicked him when he fell." Matthew examined the wound, which was still bleeding freely. He pressed the towel against Charley's head. "I'm going to have to stitch it up. Can you get my bag from the wagon, Boston?" As she hurried out, he looked at Adam. "For once his drinking might be a benefit. If he regains consciousness before I'm done, at least the alcohol might dull the pain."

But Charley did not wake up before Matthew completed the stitches.

The accident cast a pall over the party, and soon everyone but Laurina and the children drifted away. Matthew sent them home, and Adam wondered how many lonely evenings Laurina must spend with Matthew out caring for patients. He'd have to remember to pray for her and Matthew.

At almost nine that evening Charley finally awoke, coming groggily out of unconsciousness. Matthew and Adam had brought chairs from the sitting room into the bedchamber, and were talking quietly by lamplight when Charley opened his eyes and groaned.

When he'd regained consciousness enough to ask in a slurred voice where he was, Matthew told him about his accident. Charley wanted to drift off to sleep again within a few minutes, but Matthew wouldn't allow it. "Head accidents are nothing to fool with, Charley. You go to sleep again now, and you might never wake up."

Charley called his horse every name Adam had ever heard a horse called and then some, holding his head the whole while. Adam knew some of his parishioners were proficient in the use of profanity, but never before had someone used it in his house.

After a while, Adam encouraged Matthew to go home. "You should be with Laurina and the children. I can keep Charley awake for a few hours."

But Matthew stayed. "You've no one to send for me if

things take a turn for the worse."

By dawn, Charley had calmed down enough to apologize to Adam for his language the night before. The man's head was obviously still hurting horribly, and he was still blaming his horse.

"Can't fault a horse for kicking you if you put your head in the way of its hooves, Charley," Adam finally said.

"Shouldn't have tossed me off in the first place."

"Shouldn't have been drunk in the first place, Charley," Matthew said evenly. "I keep telling you, one of these days that drinking is going to be the death of you."

Charley held his head and scowled. "Aw, go on with ya. Does it say in the Ten Commandments 'Thou shalt not drink liquor'? It does not! And the Good Book even says to take a little wine for your stomach. Ain't that right, Reverend?"

"Doesn't say to take so much it isn't good for your head, Charley," Adam replied. "You're always telling me what the Bible says, Charley. Where'd you learn so much about it, anyway?"

"Guess I jest listen real good at Sabbath meetings, Reverend."

"You know, Charley, God has something better in mind for you than this kind of life."

"Aw, I like my life fine as it is. You two sound like that pesty Miss Ida Horn of the Ladies' Temperance Society. Would you believe she had the nerve to come into Thompson and Bue's Billiard Hall the other day? Strolled in as bold as you please. Wanted us gents to go to a play in Granite Falls."

"What play was that?"

Charley hunched his shoulders and mumbled. *"Ten Nights in a Bar Room."*

Matthew and Adam burst into laughter.

"It ain't funny. What's a town comin' to when a fella can't have a peaceful drink and cigar at a billiard hall without some naggin' female comin' around?" He crossed his arms and scowled as the men's laughter died down. "And jest 'cause I'm lyin' in yer bed don't give you the right to give me an extra sermon this week."

"Maybe not. But keeping me up all night to make sure you stay in the land of the living gives me the right to say anything I please. And I'm telling you that you need to accept Christ—that Man the Book you're always quoting talks so much about. Accept His love for you and tell Him you don't want to keep living as a sinner—and you'll find how good life can get."

"The words are easy, Reverend. It's givin' up the liquor that's hard."

"God will help you with that, if you'll let Him. So will Matthew and I, right, Matthew?"

"Right. And anyway, Charley, you keep drinking like this, and you're going to die real young."

Charley chuckled. "Wouldn't the ladies in this town hate that, though?"

Adam and Matthew couldn't help but smile with him.

Matthew finally allowed Charley to go to sleep, and Adam walked with Matthew to the door. Watching the sun come up over the prairie and hearing the meadowlarks greet the new day, Adam wondered why the prairie looked so lonely to him. He had loved the prairie from the first time he laid eyes on it. To others it was empty, but to him it was full of life. Beautiful flowers were tucked into the prairie grass. Gophers, prairie chickens, and meadowlarks flourished.

Lately, though, it seemed barren. Ever since Millicent left, he admitted to himself. "Draw her heart to you, Father." He repeated his constant prayer to the boom! boom! boom! of the prairie chicken and the delicate song of the lark, the sounds of the prairie awakening.

ten

Millicent listened impatiently to Thomas Wilcox tell of his latest success at the bank where he worked. He'd maneuvered a friendship with one of the officers into a convenient stepping stone, managing to convince the bank president that some of his friend's work was really his own. It had cost him a friendship, but after all, what were friendships for if not to help one succeed in business?

She wanted to tell him how despicable she found his actions. What would Adam Conrad say to him? Diplomatic Adam would probably find something good to say and manage to make the young banker feel guilty without once condemning his actions. She wished she could think of something of the sort. Instead, she just sat on the veranda with the scent of lilacs thick in the air, fanning herself in the unusual warmth, wishing Mr. Wilcox would disappear.

"Miss Millicent, are you listening to me?"

"Yes, of course. You were telling me how you received your latest promotion."

"What is most important, my dear, is that I *have* been promoted. I can afford a wife now." He reached to take her hand, and in her shock, she didn't think to draw it away. She stared at the man sitting beside her, at the smug face below the dull blonde hair.

"Pardon me?"

"I'm not surprised at your amazement. I've been

courting you for a long while now without proposing—but I wanted to have a position in which I could support you properly before asking for your hand."

Now she did have enough presence of mind to remove her hand from his, drawing herself up even straighter than usual. "Mr. Wilcox, I hardly know what to say."

He frowned and tried to take her hand once more, but she began fanning herself with her handkerchief again and avoided the unpleasant contact. "Really, dear, you must have suspected I wished to ask for your hand eventually. We've been courting for over a year."

She refrained from demanding he quit calling her dear. Bad enough to turn down his proposal; she didn't need to anger him further. "But you've never spoke of marriage before, Mr. Wilcox. I assumed you weren't ready to commit yourself."

His eyes narrowed and beneath his choppy little mustache, his full lips twitched. "You're awful strong on the rights of women. You haven't taken it into your head to follow Victoria Woodhull's thoughts on free love, have you?"

Millicent jumped to her feet. "How dare you say such a thing to me, Thomas Wilcox? Is that anything to say to a woman you're asking to marry you? Why, if I were a man, I'd. . .I'd pummel you right in your pompous little face!"

Even in the dim light, she could see how pale his face grew as he stood up. "My dear, I. . . ."

She stamped her high buttoned shoe on the wooden floor. "And don't call me dear! Any man who would ask whether I believed a woman should. . .without being married. . .and then in the very next sentence call me 'my dear'. . .!" She was losing all ability to talk coherently.

"Don't ever speak to me again!"

She stormed into the house, slamming the door behind her. Gathering her skirt, she rushed up the stairs toward her bedchamber. Halfway there, she turned and went as swiftly down and into the parlor. She plopped down on the emerald green loveseat across from Mrs. Canfield.

The older woman looked up from the book in her lap. "Do you wish to tell me about it, Millicent?"

"That man is impossible!" She crossed her legs, swinging the top leg to and fro like the pendulum on the old grandfather clock which stood next to the loveseat, her shoe peeking out from beneath her skirt.

"Mr. Wilcox?"

"Yes! He had the audacity to ask if I. . .if I believed in free love, directly after asking me to marry him!"

Mrs. Canfield's bushy white brows rose above her faded blue eyes, and spots of red brightened her round, wrinkled cheeks. "That is frightfully ungentlemanly, even for these times!"

Millicent had never seen Mrs. Canfield react so strongly to anything, and it relieved her anger as nothing else could have. Laughter welled up inside her. "I told him off properly, Mrs. Canfield, never fear." She hesitated. "Well, maybe not so properly. You should have seen his face when I told him to leave and never come back." Her laughter bubbled into the room. "I felt just like one of the heroines in a magazine serial." She pointed an arm toward the door and said dramatically, "Go! And never darken my doorstep again!"

"I'm sure there was never a heroine more justified in her anger than you. The idea, speaking to a fine woman like yourself that way!"

Millicent leaned her head against the back of the loveseat, ignoring the flattening of her curls. "You know, Mrs. Canfield, I think what truly makes me the most angry is that I don't know any young men here as fine as Matthew and Reverend Conrad."

The older woman set aside her book and moved to join Millicent on the loveseat, her dove gray dress rustling around her plump body. She took Millicent's hands in her soft round ones. "You're half in love with Reverend Conrad, aren't you?"

Millicent's eyes stung with tears. "I'm very much afraid I am, Mrs. Canfield."

"Has he spoken of his feelings for you?"

Millicent gave a shaky attempt at a laugh. "No, but he wouldn't on such short acquaintance. I'd hoped he would ask permission to correspond with me, but he didn't." Even with Mrs. Canfield, she wouldn't share Adam's love for Laurina. The secret wasn't hers to share.

The older woman patted Millicent's fingers, and Millicent was surprised to see tears in Mrs. Canfield's eyes too. Millicent dashed at hers with the back of her free hand, only to have her eyes fill again immediately. "You needn't cry for me, Mrs. Canfield. After all, how many times have I said a woman doesn't need a man to lean on?"

A tear escaped the older woman's eyes and ran down her furrowed cheek. "Oh my dear, how often I've prayed you would find a man who would make you realize what a wonderful experience love can be between a man and a woman."

"You...you prayed for me?" Millicent tried to say over the sob in her throat.

"Why of course, my dear. I've always prayed for you."

"But you never told me."

"I'm afraid I was brought up in a family that thought religious things were best kept private. I assumed you'd know I prayed for you."

Millicent laid her free hand over Mrs. Canfield's. "Well, I know now, and I'm grateful for your prayers." She took her hands away to reach for her handkerchief, and Mrs. Canfield took the opportunity to reach for her own. "My goodness, for two independent women, we've certainly given into tears, haven't we?"

When their tears were dried, Millicent said hesitantly, "Mrs. Canfield, Reverend Conrad gave me his Bible. I've been trying to read it every day, but it's like reading Greek. I've seen you reading yours often through the years, and I wondered—could you help me?"

"Oh, my dear, of course! You know, a group of women at church are starting a Bible study. Perhaps we should join. We could study our lessons together during the week, if you like."

Propped up against her pillows later that evening, Millicent turned the pages in Adam's Bible and reread by lamplight the verse he had spoken of in his sermon, Romans 10:9: "...If thou shalt confess with thy mouth the Lord Jesus, and shalt believe in thine heart that God hath raised him from the dead, thou shalt be saved."

A nagging little voice in her head urged her to postpone making a decision, but the longing to know Adam's God had only grown since leaving Chippewa City, so she grabbed her courage and took a deep breath. "Lord God, I don't know how to pray other than to say grace or the prayers we use during the church service each week, but since Thou dost already know my thoughts, I'm trusting that Thou wilt accept my words, even if they aren't in proper form. I believe that I can never be good enough to make up for all the wrong things I've done, and I believe that Thy Son Jesus lived and died for me, and that Thou raised Him from the dead as I read in the Bible. I want to know Thee, as Adam and Matthew and Mrs. Canfield know Thee, so I ask Thy help, Lord, even though I feel so unworthy. Amen."

She sat with her hands clasped on the open Bible and her eyes closed. Was she supposed to feel anything special? All she felt was relief that she'd finally made the decision to accept the Christian faith as her own. After a few moments, she reread Romans 10:9. Closing the book, she rubbed a hand over the worn cover. Then she set it on the marble-topped table beside the bed and blew out the lamp.

The Bible studies helped to make the Bible understandable, and Millicent marveled at the change. Not that she understood everything, but she could see now that as Adam had told her, the entire Book pointed the way to God through His Son Jesus. The more she learned, the more she wanted to know. She hated to put the Book aside for such mundane things as planning lessons for her classes.

When she first returned from Chippewa City, she was more thrilled with the thought that the Bible she read had belonged to Adam than she was with what it said. She still treasured the book as Adam's, but now she wondered how the verses he'd underlined had touched his life, and examined the notes he'd made in the margins for clues to further her knowledge of God.

Even church seemed different now. Before, she'd noticed only the hypocrites; now she saw the many people who showed love to each other. When she mentioned her observations to Mrs. Canfield, the wise old woman said, "Well, naturally there would have to be something right about the church. After all, Christianity has survived for almost nineteen hundred years."

Millicent and Mrs. Canfield grew closer as they studied the Bible and prayed together. At first, Millicent felt awkward praying out loud, and she thought Mrs. Canfield probably felt the same. But soon they grew comfortable praying together for the church, for each other, and for Matthew and his family. Millicent prayed for Adam and his church by herself, but she suspected Mrs. Canfield prayed for him too. She had a warm feeling of contentment knowing her prayers could touch his life even if she never could.

One night after reading a letter from Matthew and Laurina, Millicent said, "It's silly, Mrs. Canfield, but I miss Matthew more now than I did before I visited him." She picked a thread from her skirt and said thoughtfully, "I wish it weren't necessary to grow accustomed to being away from him all over again."

"It isn't necessary, child. You have no husband to keep you here. If you wish to move to Minnesota, you are free to do so."

Millicent thought of the straggling main street of Chippewa City, and a shiver of distaste ran through her. "I don't think I could stand that, Mrs. Canfield. You have no idea how primitive life is there. Why, they don't even have churches."

Mrs. Canfield leaned closer to the lamp to better see the lace collar she was mending. "A building doesn't make a church, Millicent. People do."

"Adam told me once that the church is a visible symbol to people. How can it be a visible symbol if it isn't a building?"

"The lives of the people of the church are a symbol, as is their Sabbath meeting, no matter where it takes place. Evidently you saw something there in spite of the lack of a building."

Millicent was silent for a few minutes. Finally Mrs. Canfield laid aside her mending and leaned forward, her plump, age-freckled hands folded in her lap. "I do hope you don't feel you must stay here because of me. I'll not pretend I won't miss you if you leave, but I've lived through many leave-takings in my life, and will survive fine with God and my friends for company."

Millicent shook her head. "I have no intention of moving to Chippewa City. I love the comforts and opportunities of civilization too well. Even with a bustle, the lack of upholstered furniture made me sore."

"Would you not move even for Reverend Conrad, Millicent?" the older woman asked gently.

"No." Millicent bit her bottom lip. "He said the most wonderful thing at the wedding. I don't recall the Bible verse, but it was about marriage being two people committed to the same thing. His commitment is to be part of the church's place in Chippewa City. He needs someone who can share that commitment. I couldn't make myself live there, no matter how much I care for him."

The age lines in Mrs. Canfield's face deepened. "Are you certain?"

"Yes." Millicent took a deep, shaky breath and turned the conversation in another direction. "I'm concerned for Johnny and Pearl's education, Mrs. Canfield. In Chippewa

County there are only thirteen one room common schools in the twenty-six districts. Only three school houses have the most basic supplies such as globes, maps, and dictionaries. Many of the children can't afford school books. Matthew's children will attend the Chippewa City school. I visited the school, and the instructor seems adequate, but my heart goes out to the children in the other districts."

"Each person sees more that needs to be done in this world than they alone are capable of achieving, Millicent."

"I suppose that's true." From the marble-topped table beside her, she picked up the photograph taken the day of the wedding of Matthew and his bride. Matthew insisted she have hers taken too, so he might have her likeness. The photographer charged fifty cents for two photographs, but the money was well spent. How she wished she had a photograph of Adam, also! "I'd like to go back for a visit some time," she said.

"We can always ask God to show you whether you are to go back to visit."

Millicent's heart grew lighter, and she beamed at Mrs. Canfield. "Yes, we can. Isn't it wonderful to have such a God?"

For a while they seemed to receive no answer to their prayers, and then, six weeks after she returned from Chippewa City, she received a letter from Mr. Weaver of the *Valley Ventilator*. He asked if she would reconsider a teaching position in Chippewa County. A contract for the summer term was offered, with possible renewal of the contract following that time if both sides so desired.

Mrs. Canfield agreed the letter seemed the perfect answer to their prayers, and Millicent posted an acceptance by the next day's mail. She felt no need to mention she had no intention of exercising the possible renewal option. She kept reminding herself that she was going to visit Matthew and his family. But she knew the wings on her heart were from the prospect of seeing Adam Conrad again.

eleven

Adam sat at supper with Matthew's family and drank in the sight of Millicent seated between Johnny and Pearl across the table from him. Even with the evidence of her presence in front of him, he could hardly believe she was truly here.

"So, I'll be here for the summer," she was explaining, her face shining. "Mr. Weaver says I won't be teaching at the school in Chippewa City, but at one a couple of miles out in the country. I'll be staying with Stina and Olaf. It was a relief to find I'm boarding with someone I've already met."

She was staying all summer! His heart raced in anticipation.

Matthew rubbed a fist back and forth across his jaw. "A school by Olaf and Stina's. Would that be the one the boys fixed up last winter, Adam?"

"I believe so." His stomach tied itself into a knot. Imagine Millicent, with her love of beauty and order, teaching in that shanty! If he was correct and she was the author of that letter to the editor, the experience wouldn't increase her love for the area.

She leaned forward eagerly. "Tell me about it."

"Well, there wasn't going to be a school term held in that district last winter," Matthew explained. "Most farmers and many other folk are delinquent in their property taxes due to the grasshopper years, so there's not much money to spend on schools. The building used for your school had no stove or fireplace, and wasn't sufficient against the winter weather. All the children in that district belong to farming families, and most of the boys and many of the girls need to help in the fields during the spring and summer terms—which meant a lot of the children weren't able to go to school at all. You tell her what happened, Adam."

"Some of the older boys held a wood-pile caucus. They found none of them wanted to miss out on any more school. They decided if their parents agreed, they'd fix up the school themselves. They did, and were able to have a winter term. You probably won't meet many of those boys, though, Miss Millicent, teaching a summer term."

Matthew rested his elbows on the table. "What Adam isn't telling you, Millie, is that he managed to procure a teacher for the term, and filled in himself when the teacher was ill, in addition to fulfilling his own responsibilities and helping Laurina out."

Adam felt his face grow warm. "Still, the school would never have happened without the boys."

"They're a square-toed bunch, all right," Matthew agreed.

"Millicent brought some books and other supplies for the school," Laurina offered.

"You should have seen my baggage this trip, Mr. Conrad. We couldn't have managed it all with your load of lumber in April. Along with my valises and hat boxes, I have three trunks. The stagecoach driver at Granite Falls turned as white as limestone when he saw everything! But I remembered what Chippewa City's teacher, Nettie Bartlett, said about the lack of books and teaching materials when I visited with her last time I was here, so I brought along what I could."

Stretching his long legs in front of him and clasping his hands behind his head , Matthew leaned back in his chair. "Bet you'll be the best teacher in these parts, Millie."

She flushed with pleasure. "I'm not so certain. Miss Bartlett seemed very competent. It's difficult for anyone to teach well without proper materials."

Matthew's grin filled his face, and Adam knew he must be as glad to see Millicent as he was himself. "Don't be so modest, Millie. Bet your students win the county spelling contest at the end of the term."

"I'm not so egotistical as to accept your challenge without meeting my students and learning where their present abilities lie, Matthew."

"I'm sure Matthew is right about your skill," Laurina said as she rose to clear away the dishes. "But I believe your generous, lively spirit will benefit your students most."

Adam silently agreed.

"Did you notice the lilac bush beside the front door when you arrived, Adam?" Laurina asked. "Millicent brought it all the way from Illinois. Of course, it's small yet, but it will grow."

"I hope the bush can grow here," Millicent said, laughing.

"Anything will grow here!" Matthew boasted. "Why, the black soil is so rich that a walking stick stuck in the ground would take root and grow!"

"Aunt Millicent brought Pearl and me books," Johnny interrupted.

Pearl nodded, her blonde curls bouncing. "Books."

Millicent shrugged her blue checked shoulders. "The

teacher in me, I guess."

"She said she'd help us read 'em later. Can I go to a real school, Boston, now that Aunt Millicent is here?"

"You'll begin with the summer term here in Chippewa City, Johnny," Laurina answered. "Aunt Millicent's school will be too far away for you."

Millicent accepted the plate of fresh strawberry pie Laurina handed her. "I can't believe all the building in this town in the two months I was away! The sound of hammering and sawing hasn't stopped since I arrived yesterday. There are new stores and new homes. What has happened to make it grow so fast?"

Pride filled Matthew's face. "I told you this town was going to grow, Millie. With the 'hoppers gone and the railroad coming, people are pouring into the area, and they generally stick. Why, the town fathers even laid out two new additions last week. Mr. Frink, the town's first settler, donated the land. Streets are being planned and the corner lots are selling quick."

"Civilization is coming, Miss Millicent," Adam said. "There's even a temperance league now, and the women have about convinced most people that liquor has no place in a family town." Would her attitude change after three more months here, seeing the town grow, seeing it struggle to become more like the cities of the East?

The blue eyes that had danced in his memory for the last few weeks were large as they looked into his across the table. "Perhaps I won't need to wait a century after all, Mr. Conrad," she said softly.

He felt goosebumps rise along his spine as his gaze remained locked with hers. She recalled their conversation about the town that first day. Ridiculous to be thrilled over such a little thing, he admonished himself, but the thrill lingered.

While Millicent and Laurina did the dishes, Adam and Matthew opened the windows to the cool evening breeze, hooking fly netting over the openings. Afterward, Adam seated himself where he could watch Millicent as he and Matthew talked. She was just as he remembered, but more wonderful in every way. He shouldn't have come tonight! As a minister, he knew better than to place himself unnecessarily in the midst of temptation. When he was near her, he was tempted to forget God's command not to be yoked with unbelievers.

When the women joined the men in the "parlor," Johnny begged Millicent to read him his new book, and Pearl joined in with her smile that was hard to resist.

"Have to do that tomorrow, Johnny," Matthew said as he lifted Pearl to his lap. Johnny groaned and dropped to the braided rug in front of Matthew's chair. "It's getting late, and it's time for devotions.'

Johnny perked up immediately. Adam remembered from when he and Laurina were engaged that Johnny liked what he called the Bible story time.

Since Pearl already occupied Matthew's lap, Johnny leaned against Adam's leg, and Adam lifted him to his knee. When Adam looked up, he saw Millicent's gaze resting solemnly on the boy, and he wondered what made her so sober. Was she uncomfortable about the devotional time?

He noticed she listened attentively to the reading. Afterward, Matthew told Millicent they'd started something new with their devotions since she was last there. "Yes," Johnny piped up. "We all get to say a prayer."

Matthew grinned at him. "That's right, Johnny. Who do you think should start tonight?"

"Me!" Johnny didn't wait for Matthew to agree. He closed his eyes tight, leaned back against Adam's chest and clasped his hands together hard. "Dear God, thank you for bringin' Aunt Millicent back, and thank you for the books she brought for me and Pearl. Help me learn to read real good. Please take care of Pa. Amen." He lifted his head. "It's your turn, Aunt Millicent."

Adam's gaze darted to Millicent. He'd just opened his mouth to tell her she didn't have to pray aloud if she didn't want, when she began. His eyes closed from habit as she prayed, "Father God, thank Thee for this time Thou hast allowed me to spend near my brother and his dear family. We lift this town, which is growing so quickly, before Thee, and ask that Thou wilt draw the hearts of the townspeople and farmer to Thyself. In Jesus Name, Amen."

Adam could barely believe his ears. He hardly heard the others as they prayed, wondering what Millicent's prayer meant. When Johnny poked him with his elbow and whispered impatiently, "Your turn, Adam" he simply asked God's blessing on those present, as he couldn't gather his thoughts quickly enough for a more involved prayer.

When Matthew and Laurina went to tuck the children into bed in the room that still smelled of new wood, Millicent brought Adam's Bible to him. His heart sank at the sight of it. He reached for the familiar, worn book slowly, unable to look her in the eyes for fear his disappointment would show. Her prayer must not have indicated a change of heart after all.

"When I found I'd be returning to Chippewa City, Mr. Conrad, I purchased my own Bible." His eyes shifted to hers. "You had so many notes in yours I felt you needed it. Mrs. Canfield and I joined a Bible study back in Illinois, so I really must have one of my own, you see."

"You joined a Bible study?"

She nodded, and the eyes that met his had a special glow. "I...I've accepted Christ's gift, His payment for my sins."

He swept her into his arms, barely able to contain the joy that poured through him. "Thank Thee, Lord!" he whispered huskily against her neck, the subtle scent of violets surrounding him. "Oh, thank Thee!"

He stiffened. What was he doing, hugging her like this, and in her brother's home? But she wasn't pulling way, and he loosened his hold only enough to rest his hands at her waist and search her radiant blue eyes. His heart tripped over itself. Could she possibly care for him as he cared for her?

Millicent's hands linked lightly behind his neck. "Why, Mr. Conrad, you smiled! An honest-to-goodness smile!"

twelve

Adam stepped back, his hands slipping from her waist. Millicent was still heady from the joy she saw in his eyes and the feeling of his arms about her.

"I've been praying you'd accept Him, Millicent. It's shameful to admit, but I can hardly believe He answered me so soon."

She brushed at a lock of her hair that he'd displaced and said mischievously, "It may not have been all *your* prayers, Reverend. Mrs. Canfield has been praying for me for years."

The happiness in his face continued to fill her with wonder. "I'm glad God has had someone there for you all this time." His face settled into its more accustomed sober expression, though his eyes still gleamed with pleasure. His deep voice was tinged with shyness. "May I call on you, Miss Millicent?"

She wanted to jump up and down and throw herself into his arms, but she settled for a smile. "I should like that, Mr. Conrad."

Somehow their hands had become linked, and he squeezed her fingers slightly. "Adam."

"Adam," she agreed.

He darted a glance at the children's bedchamber and released her hands suddenly as Laurina and Matthew came toward them. Millicent's joy faded. Would Laurina always be in his heart?

119

The next morning Millicent swayed on the high wagon seat beside Adam as she drank in the beauty of the June prairie. The flowers of April were gone, replaced by larkspur, prairie rose, and the violet blossoms of the ground plum. Her throat ached with the beauty before her, but she wondered if she would think it so lovely if she hadn't left herself the option of returning to the East.

She could hardly believe she was actually beside Adam again after all the weeks of longing for him. And he'd asked to call on her! Whenever their eyes met, happiness seemed to fill the prairie-scented air.

Adam nodded toward a small building, little more than a shack, still over a quarter mile away. "That's it, Miss Millicent." He turned off the ruts that served as a road to cross the unbroken land toward the schoolhouse, and Millicent grabbed the wagon seat as they bounced over the flower-filled prairie grass. "The building was just a claim shanty when the boys decided to redeem it."

Millicent was having difficulty now keeping hold of her parasol while trying to stay on the wagon seat. "What is a claim shanty?"

"A building thrown up to satisfy the legal requirements for a homestead claim. The builder doesn't expect it to be his home for long, and the quality reflects that expectation."

A black ribbon slashed through the green prairie between them and the school. "That's a ditch the neighboring farmers dug last fall to save the schoolhouse from a prairie fire," he told her. "It worked that time. Sometimes it doesn't."

Millicent's excitement died as they came to a rocking

halt in front of the building. Even Adam's touch as he helped her down didn't take her attention from the make-shift schoolhouse. She stared at it in dismay. Why hadn't Mr. Weaver told her the kind of place where she'd be teaching? She'd known from the men's comments yesterday this wouldn't be one of the district's best schools, but this was ridiculous. Anger welled up in her. The old goat probably thought he was being smart, taking revenge for her winning the crowd's favor in their discussion of women's rights. He was likely expecting her to come hurrying to his office, begging him to give her another assignment. She lifted her chin; she wouldn't give him the pleasure. "It's only three months," she said, stalking toward the door.

"Pardon?"

She forced a smile. "At least it's not built of sod."

"No. Hand-sawed cottonwood planks, and covered with plaster the boys made themselves." He opened the board door, and Millicent clung to her courage as she entered the small building.

The single room had two windows. On one wall was a blackboard, literally wide boards painted black, not the slate to which she was accustomed. In the rear of the room, an old cook stove with a large cast-iron drum served for heat. The furnishings were crude, not the patented desks she'd had in her classroom back East.

Adam cleared his throat. "The boys made the seats, desks, and teacher's desk themselves."

She nodded, not trusting her voice, and walked slowly around the tiny room. Only three months, she reminded herself, aware Adam was watching her reactions. If Mrs. Canfield could only see this place, the older woman would realize why she couldn't move here permanently, even for Adam. She stared out one of the uncurtained windows. "I'll need fly netting for the windows if I'm to keep the building properly aired." Why did her voice have to wobble?

"Before it was repaired, there were holes in the wall large enough for a skunk to crawl through. The boys had to cut through the frost of a Minnesota winter to get this clay. They hauled water and heated it in kettles on the stove to thaw the clay after they got it here. They boiled water and mixed the clay with slough hay before chinking the holes and plastering both the inside and outside of the building." Adam ran his long fingers over the wavy, dingy plaster. "The building may not be elegant, but no teacher anywhere has more eager students, Miss Millicent."

Her eyelids burned from the tears his words brought. Had she ever wanted anything so much she'd fight that hard for it? "You're right, Adam. Pray God I'll be able to meet the challenge." She took a deep breath. "I thought I'd need to clean, but there's barely a speck of dirt."

"I expect when they heard you were coming, the students readied the building for you. I'll speak with the school board members and urge them to dig a well and build outhouses immediately."

She saw a muscle jerk in his cheek, and realized he too was angry with Mr. Weaver for not telling her the details of the position she'd accepted. "Well, I wanted to become better acquainted with the Lord. It looks like I'll be leaning on Him a lot this summer!"

A flash of joy brightened his face. "He can take a lot of leaning."

They carried the books Millicent had brought from

Illinois and piled them on the uneven top of the teacher's desk, since there were no shelves. "School books are sold at the mercantile, but many of the students can't afford them," Adam told her. The globe she'd brought went on the desk also, and Adam helped her tack up a reading chart and some Camp's outline maps.

She stood in the doorway as they left and looked back into the room with a satisfied smile. It looked much more like a school room now.

Adam's hand rested on her shoulder as he stood behind her. "I'm glad you came back, Millicent."

She longed to lean her cheek against his strong, tanned fingers and tell him how he'd filled her dreams since April. But she said only, "I'm glad too."

Adam left her and one of her trunks, along with a valise and some hatboxes, at Stina and Olaf's before going on his way to visit ill parishioners. Millicent regretted leaving some of her clothing at Matthew's, but she knew Stina's house would have little room for all her things.

The house seemed too crowded at first, filled with Stina, Olaf, and their five children; she'd never lived with so many people before, but their sincere welcome soon put her at ease. She shared a room with the three girls, who ranged in age from ten to fifteen. The long, narrow room had a bunk-style bed on each end, built into the wall and rosmalled, painted with swirling red and gold patterns against a dark green background. It was a style from the Telemarken area of Norway, according to the girls, and painted by Stina. The designs brightened the otherwise simple room. The mattresses looked unusual, however, and Millicent wasn't reassured to find they were muslin sacks stuffed with dried prairie grass.

Thorburn, whom she remembered from the room raising, was at sixteen the oldest child. He was friendly
without being pushy. When he wasn't doing chores, she
usually saw him with his nose in a worn Norwegian-
English dictionary. "I k-nowed and k-nifed for months
before Ellie told me the k's are silent," he said with a
sheepish grin. Ellie was the girl with the long brown braid
that Millicent remembered at Matthew's room raising.

Two days after Millicent first saw the schoolhouse, the
summer term began. With the Anderson girls and Anders,
the ten-year-old boy, she walked the mile to the school,
carrying her grade book and lunch pail, her parasol over
her head. They took turns carrying the bucket of fresh
water the students would need.

The children chattered along the way, excited to start the
term and see the other children in the district. Millicent
was sure they were no more eager than she was for this day,
though she wished fervently she needn't walk through the
fields. Insects jumped on her legs beneath skirts that
snagged stickers, while the rich soil of which Matthew
spoke so highly clung to her hem. How was she ever going
to keep her clothes clean, living here?

A few students had arrived before them. They had piled
Millicent's desk with prairie roses, and her chest swelled
at their welcome.

Fourteen students attended that morning, mostly girls
and young boys, ranging in age from six to seventeen.
None of the older boys who had so earnestly readied the
school during the winter were present. Millicent carefully
listed the names of the fourteen in her grade book, then

began the day with the same morning prayer she'd used in her classes back East. Only now, she trusted the God to whom she prayed.

The students looked surprised when she told them to stand beside their desks so they could do calisthenics, but they obeyed. They followed her example as she led them through the simple stretching exercises modern education considered beneficial to a student's day. As always, Millicent wished fashion didn't insist on her corset and bodice fitting so tightly; they made both the exercises and the necessary increase in breathing difficult.

Only four of the students had school books, three having readers and one, whose father didn't believe in exposing his children to the "fairy tales" in the readers, a *United States History*. The hunger in the students' eyes as they shared the books she'd brought won Millicent's heart.

She listened patiently as each student stood and read a sample for her. The disparity in ability was appalling to her, as she was accustomed to teaching only one grade. How was she going to teach such a variety of reading levels? To make matters worse, a number of the children, such as the Lindstroms, were able to read little English, which wasn't their native language. "I can do all things through Christ, who strengtheneth me"; she encouraged herself with the verse from Philippians even as she smiled encouragingly at the student stumbling over the word "briar."

At lunch time, Millicent joined the students outside, donning the sunbonnet Laurina had lent her. The cold boiled potato and thick slices of bread with butter filled her growling stomach.

The children had just settled down to begin the afternoon arithmetic lesson when Ellie hurried into the room, spots of excitement reddening her cheeks. "I'm sorry to be late, Ma'am, but Father says I can only come to school in the afternoons—that is, if I get my house and field chores done in the mornings."

Millicent nodded to her, wondering how she'd find time to work the reading and history lessons of the morning into Ellie's half-days while teaching arithmetic and science to her and the other students in the afternoons. "We'll be glad to have you, Ellie, and hope you can be with us every afternoon." She turned to Stina's eldest girl, Sonneva. "Would you share your desk with Ellie?" The girls crowded together at the makeshift desk.

Millicent was further surprised when Thorburn came in halfway through the arithmetic lesson, followed by another older boy named Lars Arnsted. Both boys were dusty and somewhat odorous, but their faces were eager. Their parents had agreed they could attend school for a limited amount of time each week. Millicent knew from Matthew and Adam's comments that this was a great luxury for the boys, and she was determined to teach them everything possible during those precious hours.

The children needed to be convinced that the school day had come to an end. They drifted off in groups of two or three, loathe to leave their friends and the wonderful books.

As Millicent swept the floor, she made plans for the next day's classes. If she kept Ellie and the older boys inside during the afternoon recess, she would have a few more minutes with them. She wondered how much time they would have to spend on homework, knowing they had evening as well as morning chores. The boys had said they wouldn't be able to come every day, so her time with them would be even more limited.

She was so lost in her plans that she didn't hear the mule drawn wagon creak into the cut prairie grass in front of the school, and she almost dropped her broom when Adam entered the building. "I hope I'm not intruding. I thought you needed some light in here." He held up a kerosene lamp that could be hung from the ceiling.

"Oh, Adam, thank you! With only two windows, I'm sure we'll need the light." Joy at the sight of him rose within her like bubbles in a soda fountain drink.

While he attached the lamp to the ceiling, she chattered about her day, telling him of the students and their varying abilities, the older boys, and Ellie. "Ellie seems exceptionally intelligent. It's a shame she can't spend more time at school. I wonder whether her father would allow her to come mornings also, if I spoke to him."

Adam stepped down from the wobbly wooden bench he was using for a stool. "I wouldn't recommend it. He's set in his ways and has quite a temper."

A frown creased her forehead. "Surely you don't think he'd harm me for suggesting his daughter get more education."

"He isn't a man I'd trust to be reasonable, Miss Millicent. His temper is well-known in these parts, and he has definite ideas on women and education. He makes Art Weaver look like a supporter of women's rights."

"I see. Then I'll just do the best I can in the time Ellie has available."

"I spoke to the school board about the well and outhouses. They called a special meeting last night to vote on them. You'll have them both as soon as the board can hire someone to dig them."

Millicent propped her hands on her rose and blue striped skirt. "Adam Conrad, I expect you are being as modest as usual about your part in convincing them to spend the money." She laughed as his cheeks turned dusky red above the black beard. "I can see I guessed right. And Mr. Weaver was probably the hardest to convince of them all."

He didn't confirm her suspicion, but one corner of his mouth turned up. The sight of it did funny things to her stomach. What would it be like to have his lips touch hers? She'd only been kissed once, when Thomas Wilcox caught her unexpectedly. She hadn't liked it, but she suspected she would feel differently with Adam. Her gaze moved to his eyes, and she saw her own feelings reflected in his. His breath was ragged as he tore his gaze from hers and started toward the door. "I brought some cottonwood slips from the river to plant. Where would you like them?"

"Cottonwood slips?" she asked breathlessly, embarrassed that he had apparently read her unseemly thoughts. She followed him outside to see the small plants. She wouldn't be here to see them grow, but that fact did not take away her joy in them.

"May I drive you to the Lindstroms'?" he asked when the young trees were planted.

The walk wasn't far, but the high-heeled, high-buttoned shoes that bound her ankles made the prospect unappealing after spending most of the day on her feet. Besides, she relished the few extra minutes with him that the ride would allow, so she agreed, warmed by the gladness in his face as he helped her up to the high seat.

The school board was true to its word, and the next week's

lessons were taught to a background of workmen and mules as the well and outhouses were dug. As the men cleared an area for the well, Millicent was surprised when they uncovered a door in the ground. It opened on a deep, dank hole that must have been a root cellar at one time. The prairie had reclaimed it until the workmen discovered it.

She was relieved when the work was complete; water no longer had to be hauled from the Lindstroms' well, and the slop bucket was no longer needed.

Never had Millicent taught better behaved students. They were seldom inattentive, and the punishments she had to administer were mild and far between, usually for overexcited youngsters who forgot they were not to speak unless spoken to.

Students brought her gifts plucked on their way to school, and her desk was filled daily with new offerings of prairie roses, larkspur, and a yellow flower she couldn't identify. In spite of the difficulties of trying to teach so many levels at once, Millicent had never been so rewarded by her teaching. She only wished she had adequate supplies for these students.

Saturday evenings and Sunday afternoons were spent with Adam, and occasionally he stopped at the school or the Lindstroms' when his duties brought him near. She marvelled that he continued to be the wonderful person she'd thought him at first. In the past, young men's faults came quickly to light after a few hours spent in their company.

Millicent soon wished Ellie were able to attend classes more often, and not just for Ellie's sake but for her own also. The young woman was the fastest learner of all the students, and far more advanced in every area than the others. Millicent began having her practice penmanship while listening to the younger pupils read, writing down the stories they read on a slate. Meanwhile, Millicent had the chance to work with other students.

Millicent soon learned she could expect the older boys to attend on rainy days, and she planned lessons in advance for these days. Occasionally a boy would wander in late on a sunny afternoon, but that was rare.

Thorburn was the older boy most likely to attend, but then, he lived the closest. Besides, Millicent knew that his parents, especially Stina, were eager for him to learn as much as possible as he neared manhood. Many evenings after supper when the evening chores were done, Millicent would find him reading, though she knew he was exhausted from the day's hard work. He told her he practiced his arithmetic while he worked the fields, reciting his sums in his mind.

She thought this such an innovative idea that she encouraged the other older boys to try it. Soon they were moving ahead with their arithmetic at incredible speeds. Millicent rejoiced at the ways the Lord was answering her prayers for the students.

As attentive a student as Thorburn was, Millicent often noticed his gaze roaming to Ellie. Occasionally, when both could complete their chores early enough, he and Ellie would eat lunch together. Their joy in each other's company was plain to see.

Millicent was surprised when the last week of June, Ellie was absent for three days. Although she often slid into her seat after afternoon lessons began, she had never been absent before. Millicent was concerned the girl might be ill, but her fears were relieved when Ellie arrived on Thursday a few minutes after lunch.

Millicent moved quietly to Ellie's desk while Anders recited his sums and whispered to her to remove her sunbonnet. The girl looked at her lap and replied that she was feeling a chill and preferred to leave it on. After all, thought Millicent, perhaps Ellie was recovering from an illness.

Millicent stayed after school to work on the examination she was planning for the next week. When she opened the door for some fresh air, Thorburn's angry voice surprised her. "We *must* get married, Ellie. I'll not allow your father to do this to you again. When you are my wife, he'll have no right to touch you. We will elope Saturday."

Millicent stepped outside and stopped short at the sight before her. Ellie's bonnet was slid back on her shoulders, and Thorburn's big, calloused hands cradled her face. An ugly purple and yellow bruise was on her temple.

thirteen

Ellie gasped and drew back, hurriedly pulling her sunbonnet up to hide her face. Thor put an arm about her, and the look he shot at Millicent warned her not to hurt Ellie further.

Millicent caught back the cry that formed in her throat, remembering from her training that teachers should remain calm in all circumstances. She forced her voice to sound matter-of-fact. "Did your father do this, Ellie?"

Ellie bit her lip.

"Thor?"

The young giant glowered at her.

Millicent sent up a quick prayer for guidance. She took a deep breath and linked her fingers together, hoping they would read from her pose that she was no threat to them. "Ellie, I only want to help."

"No one can help!"

The anger and hopeless in Ellie's voice cut Millicent's heart. "God can help."

"He hasn't so far." Thor's words were as angry as his burning blue eyes.

Millicent kept her voice calm. "We'll see." She turned back to Ellie. "Are you going to elope with Thor?"

Ellie didn't reply, but Thorburn's square jaw jutted. "You may be able to stop us this time, Miss Strong, but it'll only mean another beating for Ellie. And we'll elope the next chance we get." His Norwegian accent was stronger than ever in his anger.

"I'll not tell anyone of your plans," Millicent said quietly. "But are you truly ready to marry?"

Ellie continued to chew her lip, and Thorburn drew her closer against him as he glared at Millicent. Neither answered her. "Marrying is something you should do because it's what you both want most in the world—not because you want to escape a difficult situation." Millicent put a gentle hand on Ellie's arm. "I've seen the affection you and Thor have for each other. Do you really wish to begin life under such a burden?"

"It's better than leaving Ellie where she is."

"Perhaps, Thorburn. But where would you live? How would you support her?"

"There is still some land available to homestead."

"Could you afford the cost of tools or oxen to work the land?" When he didn't reply, she continued. "I know that your situation is difficult, Ellie. But if you can find the strength to stay a while longer, I promise to try to find a way to help you that won't jeopardize your future happiness."

Ellie turned to look up into Thor's face. Her voice was small as she said, "Maybe she's right, Thor."

His fingers squeezed the blue checkered gingham covering her shoulder. "I don't want your father to hurt you again, Ellie."

"He'll be sorry now and leave me alone for a while. He always does. And if Miss Strong can't find a way to help, we can marry later."

"Ellie. . .."

Millicent held her breath as Ellie stopped him with a small hand on his workshirt. "Thor, I want it to be good when we marry. A happy time."

"I would be happy with you now, Ellie."

"I want to wait."

Thor swallowed hard. "We'll do as you wish, for now. But if your father touches you again, I will take you away from there immediately."

Millicent let out her breath with a silent thank you to God. Thor stooped to pick up the books he and Ellie had left on the ground beside them. "I'll be praying for you and working on an answer, I promise," Millicent said as they turned to leave. She hoped she hadn't promised too much. Would God answer her? Would she be able to hear His answer?

The Fourth of July dawned sunny and hot, but the heat didn't dampen the spirits of Chippewa County's residents. Most of the towns businesses were closed for the day, and many of the farmers took the day off too. After all, this was the celebration of the beginning of their wonderful nation, where all men are created equal, and all dreams are possible. Besides, crops were looking "dandy." Corn was more than knee high already.

Millicent wished Thorburn, Lars, and the other older boys were taking the day off also. They deserved a day of play after all their efforts at school and home. Yet she knew the time they spent working in their fathers' fields today would allow them more time in school next week, and more than ever she admired their commitment to their education.

The town was packed with people, and excitement filled every face. Adam and Millicent joined Matthew's family for most of the day. On First Street, as the citizens were beginning to call the ramshackle business section, they could barely make their way through the crowds. One of the stores had a cut pine tree on its boardwalk, the limbs covered with small flags. "The town didn't celebrate the Fourth last year, what with the damage from the 'hoppers," Adam told Millicent. "I guess they're making up for it now."

"It barely resembles the town as I first saw it," she told him, leaning into the arm that had captured her white gloved hand and lifting her face nearer to his to make herself heard. She could hardly believe she was to spend the entire day with him! The thought of leaving him behind when she returned to Illinois at the end of the term was growing more and more painful. A part of her was ashamed for not telling him she could never live in this country, but again and again another part of her pushed the guilt away. Today she would forget she ever had to leave, and enjoy this day with him as though it would last forever.

"The town has changed," Adam agreed.

None of the buildings that were boarded up in April looked deserted now. New boards on unfinished buildings were bright in the morning sun, and fresh paint glistened from several store fronts. Even the Chippewa City House was improving its appearance. She'd read in the newspaper that the owner wanted to be ready to compete with the Granite Falls hotels when the railroad reached town. Would the owner have a restaurant and serve oysters, as the Granite Falls' hotel did, she wondered.

In spite of the noise of the celebrants, and the horses and wagons that filled the street, some sounds she had grown used to were missing. After several minutes, she realized which noises were now quiet—the banging and sawing on new buildings, the ringing hammers from the two blacksmith shops, and the clang of the wheelwright shop. They'd taken a holiday too.

Adam pointed to an empty lot they were passing. "A shoemaker will start building here next week. As an inducement to settle here, Mr. Frink has given him the lot free of charge for his home and shop."

Millicent lifted her blue skirt and petticoat to reveal the pointed tip of a scuffed and dusty shoe. "I think he shall do a landslide business. I don't know how people are able to keep themselves in shoes in this land."

A smile touched Adam's lips. "If that news cheers you so, the news of Miss Ida Horn opening a millinery in the general store should make you ecstatic."

Surprise stopped her steps. "Is Miss Horn going to run the millinery and also keep up the work for the Ladies' Temperance League?"

"She's hoping the town will soon vote to go dry, and her duties for the Temperance League will not be so strenuous."

"Hmph!" Millicent turned quickly to find Mr. Weaver all but standing on the hem of her short train. "Miss Horn is probably right, worse luck. Only seventeen drunks in town yesterday. That's all I could see from the window of the newspaper office anyway. Town's becoming downright Easternized."

A laugh sprang from Millicent's lips. "I think I can quite safely say Chippewa City has a few days before that happens."

"How are the students, Miss Strong?" His face was carefully bland.

She gripped the handle of her white parasol and gave him a sugary smile, determined not to let him know how angry his assignment had made her. "I've never had more eager students, Mr. Weaver. However, I shan't take you up on that offer in your ad to preempt a quarter section of land. Why, I'd surely not have time to plant trees or raise the winter's provisions."

She thought she actually heard Adam chuckle, a deep, throaty sound that encouraged her to further boldness. "As to the two or three hundred in capital you recommend a school ma'am bring, I can see now the reason. On the miserly salary I'm paid, no teacher would ever be able to accumulate such a fortune *after* she came to this land."

The patronizing look she so despised was back on the man's whisker-framed face. "Now, Miss Strong, we do have some benefits to compensate for the salary. Women are allowed to vote on school issues in this state, and married women are even allowed to teach."

"At the same rate of pay as when they're single, no doubt—which is a good deal less than the rate of male teachers."

"Speaking of marriages, Miss Strong, are you planning for that last item in my ad—a fall wedding?"

fourteen

She stopped short in her tracks and stared at him coldly. How dare he ask such a thing when she was standing here on Adam's arm? She could feel that arm tense, and her anger rose. "You are no gentleman, Mr. Weaver."

The editor went off chuckling. Millicent could not look at Adam. He leaned down to ask, "Is the idea so offensive, Millicent?"

The brass band announced the beginning of the procession through First Street, relieving her of the necessity of a response. Millicent tingled with excitement as the music makers came into view. They were followed by the Old Settlers, who had been here a decade, give or take a couple years. Then came the community's societies: the Templars, the Free Masons, and the Ladies' Temperance League. The highlight of the procession, however, was a wagon drawn by six white horses with thirty-eight young women representing the states of the Union.

"There were so many people in the procession, I wonder that there was anyone left to watch it!" Millicent said to Adam as they hurried toward the grove beside the river. Millicent was glad that many of the day's festivities were to be held in that shady, park-like setting. The trees' shade was much cooler than her parasol's small shadow, and beneath the trees she would be safe from any danger of the sun reaching her skin. She hadn't been able to force herself to wear a sunbonnet to the celebration, not when she was to be with Adam the entire day.

The programme began with a prayer given by Adam, thanking God for a land in which people were free to worship Him in the manner they preferred, and asking Him to make the day one of blessing and fellowship. "We have a double reason for celebrating Independence Day, Miss Millicent," he whispered in her ear as Mr. Moyer, the owner of the bank, began to read the Declaration of Independence.

She gave him a puzzled frown.

He drew her hand through his arm and smiled. "We have liberty in Christ now. The Bible tells us that when Christ shall set thee free, thou shalt be free indeed."

"Yes." She returned his smile, and contentment filled her. Life seemed new since she had found Christ's liberty.

Following another reading of the Declaration by Olaf in Norwegian, a group of students from Miss Bartlett's school sang "America." The Chippewa City Brass Band accompanied the crowd in a rousing rendition of "Yankee Doodle" that the newspaper later said "likely scared for good the prairie chickens for miles around."

Once the programme was over, Millicent announced that chances on a log cabin quilt made by the women of the church would be available for purchase throughout the day, with the winner to be drawn before the fireworks display that evening. The funds were to go toward the establishment of a town lending library.

The announcement surprised Adam. "I didn't know there were plans afoot for a library."

"I convinced the women the town needs one. The lack of books here is shameful. How are the town's children to become civilized without books?"

"And was the raffle your idea, too?"

"Yes. It thought it up in self defense. The other women wished to have a hug social."

"A hug social?"

"They're all the novelty to raise funds for churches, haven't you heard, Reverend? The women of the church sell hugs; one hug for ten cents, three for twenty-five, and twelve for a dollar."

She couldn't read the expression on his face, and his even tone when had spoken gave no clue to his feelings on the topic. The parasol rotated slowly above her head as she began walking, trying to appear casual as she looked about at the people, at anyone other than Adam. "It was more of a veto, actually. I refused to be a part of such a thing." Just the thought of Charley Bender demanding a hug sent shivers down her spine.

They walked in silence for a few yards. Adam cleared his throat. "I'm glad you won't be selling you embraces"

"My hugs belong only to the man I love, and are not for sale at any price."

His eyes on her felt like a hot touch against her face. "Millicent—"

"Adam, are you goin' to see the horse race?" Johnny slid to a stop beside them. "The winner gets an Eagle! One day I'm goin' to have a horse that runs like the wind and win that Eagle."

Adam squeezed her hand before dragging his gaze from hers. "A ten dollar gold piece is a fine prize, all right," he answered Johnny.

Matthew, Laurina, and Pearl were close behind Johnny, and soon they all went to watch the horse racing at the track beside the baseball field.

After the race, Charley entertained the crowd by attempting to somersault over six horses. He was cheered on by a large group of men who loudly made bets on his chances, while women exclaimed in horror at the danger. With his usual swagger, Charley stopped in front of Millicent to ask if he might wear a favor as the knights of old, but she refused him, trying to control a shudder as she stepped closer to Adam. Charley had been trying to court her since the first Saturday after her arrival in June.

Charley's acrobatic attempt failed, and Matthew was put into service. Adam helped him set Charley's broken arm while Millicent waited patiently.

After Charley regained his color, he winked at Millicent. "Hows about goin' to the dance with me tonight, Miss Millie? The Reverend here don't cotton to dancin'. And besides, you owe me."

Millicent laid a gloved hand against the frills of her white blouse in surprise. "I owe you, Mr. Bender?"

He nodded, wincing as the motion jerked his arm. "Yep. If you'd given me a favor, I would of made it over those horses."

She couldn't help but laugh.

"So will you step out with me?"

She shook her head. "I'm a school ma'am, remember? I have to be in class early tomorrow morning."

"Well, don't you go sayin' 'yes' to marryin' this prim and proper old preacher before you give me a chance, Miss Millie. Woman like you needs someone lively to spice up her life."

Millicent' face burned. She turned without a word and headed toward the ball field, trying to walk in as dignified a manner as possible. Why did everyone insist on speaking of marriage today?

Adam had never spoken of marriage, and she'd used that fact to salve her conscience whenever she felt guilty for seeing him. As long as she was intent on returning to the East, their relationship would never be able to grow to love's natural fulfillment of a life together as man and wife. She couldn't live in this land, and she wasn't going to allow her attraction to Adam lure her away from her good sense. Too many of her friends had let love lead them into awful marriages.

Because they didn't praise God with one heart and one mind, said a small voice inside her. Why should those words come to mind? She and Adam both loved God; the verse had nothing to do with them.

Before long Matthew's family and Adam joined her at the ball field, and the game between the Chippewa City Club and the Cascades of Granite Falls began. The hundreds of spectators cheered their teams on until they were hoarse, even Adam joining in the shouts. In the end, Chippewa City was the winner, thirty-three runs to twenty-seven. Millicent wished the older boys from her school could have been there to see the game.

Back at the grove, Millicent thanked those who participated in the raffle for launching the library, and congratulated them on beginning such a farsighted plan on Independence Day. Mr. Weaver surprised her by offering to donate copies of *Tom Sawyer* and *My Winter on the Nile* to begin the library's collection, and Adam offered *Pope's Poems*. Mrs. Moyer said she had a copy of *The Young Lady's Book* she'd be glad to contribute.

"I'm overwhelmed by your response," Millicent was finally able to break in to say. She spread her hands palms up in helplessness. "But we have no place to keep the volumes yet." She spied Mr. Moyer in the crowd. "I'm sure our illustrious bank owner will be able to help us locate a place, however." Mr. Moyer's eyes widened with surprise, and Millicent put on her most innocent face. "You're such a knowledgeable businessman. Won't you help us locate a home for the library?"

She really wasn't fair to pick him out in the crowd on the most patriotic day of the year, but she got the result she'd hoped for.

Mr. Moyer glanced about at the crowd. "Yes. Well." He pulled his handkerchief from his jacket pocket and mopped his face. "Harumph! I. . .I see no reason we couldn't keep the books at the bank. My employees can keep track of the borrowers." His nervousness changed to pleasure and then to pride as the crowd applauded.

Millicent thanked him graciously before announcing the winner of the log cabin quilt—Charley Bender. Hoots and cat calls from the crowd didn't bother Charley, nor the suggestion called out by the owner of the billiard hall that Charley should be looking for a wife, now that he'd started his hope chest. Millicent hoped no one else saw the wink he gave her as he replied in his loud voice that he was "jest gettin' started on that little detail."

Clouds began filling the sky as twilight settled in, but the rains held off. At nine o'clock, fireworks were set off from the bridge, and the spectators thrilled to the sights and sounds. While all eyes were on the sky, Adam's arms stole around Millicent's waist, and she leaned back contentedly against his chest. The crowd gasped at an especially unusual burst of light, and Adam's beard tickled her ear as he whispered against her hair, "That's what you do to my heart, Millicent." A warm, sweet joy filled her.

Matthew lent Adam his buggy to see Millicent home to Stina and Olaf's. She leaned against Adam's arm in the luxury of padded comfort and relative privacy, as the buggy's lanterns swung gently with the horse's rhythm. She was wondrously happy with the success of the day and the joy of being alone with him.

They were still over a mile from the Lindstroms' when the storm hit with sudden ferocity. They hurried to roll down the canvas curtains, but even so the rain soaked them. The wind whipped the lanterns, and although they still burned, they were no help to the horse in finding the road. The buggy swayed precariously from the wind and the animal's unsure footing.

Millicent was surprised when Adam pulled to a stop, grabbed one of the lanterns, and helped her down from the buggy. She reached out to him, however, and ducked her head against the pelting rain as he led her quickly through the dark. He let go of her hand to yank open a heavy door before urging her inside.

She looked about her in the light of the lantern, its greasy smell filling the small building. The walls were a dingy white, and dirty, ripped cheesecloth hung from the dirt ceiling. A rusting stove stood in the middle of the room, beside a rickety oak table and equally rickety bench. "Adam, where are we?"

"About a mile from the Lindstroms' at the sod house where Johnny and Pearl's parents lived. When the storm lets up, we can continue." He was digging in a wooden box, and stood up with his hands full of twisted hay, which he used to start a fire in the stove. "Might as well try to dry out some."

Millicent set her drawstring purse and wet hat on the table and walked slowly within the circle of light, peering at the simple building that smelled like moist earth. "Is this where Laurina lived with Johnny and Pearl before she married Matthew?"

"Yes." He brushed his hands against each other to remove the particles of hay stuck to them. "I'll be back in a minute. I'm going to try to get the horse and buggy into the barn."

She pushed the door shut behind him against the lashing rains and sank to the bench beside the table. The place was more primitive than the schoolhouse where she taught. At least the school had a wooden floor. This had only a few planks placed piecemeal about the room. She looked up at the cheesecloth encased ceiling. Would the dirt roof hold up beneath the rains? The room did seem surprisingly snug against the winds.

The stove was beginning to put out warmth, and she stood before it, shaking the dampness from her skirt. Mud covered her high-buttoned shoes and the hems of her skirt and petticoat. She'd just loosened her drenched curls when Adam entered with the remaining lantern from the carriage. Water ran from the wide brim of his hat; he placed it near the stove to dry, and pulled off his soaked jacket.

Using a side comb, Millicent began to detangle her curls as the rain plunked a tune against the stove pipe that poked through the sod roof. She was aware of Adam watching in silence. "May I help?" he asked, holding out his hand as she came to a snarl.

She hesitated, then handed him the comb and turned her back to him so he could work at the tangled curls. His hands were gentle, and soon the dank room, the rain, and the entire world ceased to exist for her as she closed her eyes and surrendered to the warmth flowing through her at the intimacy of his hands in her hair, their touch at the back of her neck.

"Your hair is beautiful, Millicent." His deep voice sent vibrations through her stronger than the thunder booming over the sod roof. His hands on her shoulders burned through her white cotton blouse as he turned her to face him and drew her against his chest. "So beautiful," he whispered against her lips before covering them with his own.

His arms folded around her as gently as a bird covering its young, and she nestled contentedly in them, giving herself completely to his kisses. Eventually his lips moved from hers to explore her face; when she whispered his name, she felt him tremble as her arms slipped around his shoulders.

"I love you, Millicent." His breath was warm in her hair. "Could you ever love a sober old man like me?"

Laughter bubbled up in her and filled the room. She took his lean, bearded face between her hands. "Could I ever? Why, Adam, I've loved you almost since we met."

She watched joy follow disbelief across his face, and then he caught her so tightly to him that she gasped. He loosened his hold immediately, looking stricken, and she snuggled against his chest to reassure him. She shouldn't be with him like this, not when she knew she couldn't commit herself to spending her life with him. Yet surely a few minutes in his arms couldn't hurt. "With eyes that speak as eloquently as yours, you could never be a sober old man, Adam."

His fingers played with the curls at the back of her neck, sending shivers of delight through her, and his soft beard caressed her temple. "And have you heard those eyes ask whether you will marry me, Millicent Strong?"

fifteen

Adam's heart beat hard against her cheek. Her own heart felt as though it would explode. It was too soon! Too soon for him to ask her to marry and spoil the joy of being with him. Too soon to face the guilt of not telling him earlier that she could never live on the edge of the frontier. How could she make herself say the words that would close his arms forever?

The fingers at the back of her neck stopped moving. "Millicent?"

The dread in his one word tore at her heart and conscience. Pulling away from him, she turned and looked about the dreary sod house as she rubbed her arms, suddenly cold.

"It's very easy to see why you and Matthew love Laurina. I could never have lived here, not even for Johnny and Pearl. You deserve to share your life with someone as wonderful as Laurina."

"A person never has to do more than God asks of them, Millicent. He didn't ask you to care for Johnny and Pearl, or live in this house. What He did ask of you hasn't been easy—teaching at that ill-built schoolhouse with meager supplies, living without the comforts to which you're accustomed. It took courage for you to agree to that."

She avoided the arms that reached for her and closed her own tightly over her chest, crushing the damp lace. "It's not the same, Adam. I'm only here for the summer. Don't you see? I can walk away from everything."

Lines seemed to grow on his face as he stared across the room at her, aging him before her eyes. "Can you, Millicent? Can you walk away when the summer term is over?"

Tears stung the back of her eyelids. Why did he make her say it? "I have to, Adam." Would she ever forget his pain-bruised eyes? She sank to the bench. The lantern flame sent grotesque shadows darting over the dingy walls.

"Why can't you stay, Millicent?" His question was gentle. He brought himself down to her level, resting on his heels, searching her eyes for the truth. She reached slowly to slide her fingers through his hair and frame his face with her hands. "Your prairie is beautiful, Adam. The flowers that fill it so abundantly are a treasure I could never have imagined. And when the sun's rays tinge the grasses with a red-gold sheen at sunset, the land looks like liquid copper. But I want to live in a normal world, Adam. Do you remember the letter the school teacher wrote to the editor? I wrote that letter."

"I know."

His admission shocked her into silence. "H. . .how?"

He lifted his hands in a shrug. "Little things."

She stood up and paced the small room. "I didn't want you to know. I want to love this place, because you love it. But I like the comfort, cleanliness, and convenience of civilization. I like furniture that's upholstered, draperied windows, papered walls, carpeted floors, and a featherbed at the end of the day. I want to live where there are boardwalks and streets that are lit by gas lamps at night, not just ruts in the land. I want water piped into my house, and railroads to travel on and bring merchandise to my stores." She stopped in front of him. "I want. . .I want my children to go to school in a decent building, furnished with modern teaching materials."

"Maybe we could move. . . ."

"No." She shook her head. "Do you remember what you said at Matthew and Laurina's wedding? You prayed that they would glorify God with one heart and one mouth. We could never have that kind of unity. You feel God has called you to be a part of His work in Chippewa City. You couldn't leave, and I would despise living here. Eventually we'd grow to hate each other. I would hate you for forcing me to live here, or you would hate me for forcing you to leave the work God has given you."

His face softened. "Like so many of your friends who hate the lives they were forced into by the men they married?"

"Yes." The bitterness in her voice surprised him.

"I learned a lot about marriage from you at Matthew and Laurina's wedding, Millicent. Until I heard you tell of your friends' marriages, I never realized the extent of trust it requires for a woman to marry—to place herself and all her worldly goods into a man's hands. No wonder God compares the relationship between Himself and those who believe in Him to a marriage." This time she didn't pull away when he rested his hands on her shoulders. His deep voice softened. "I would cherish your trust, but only if you gave it joyfully, not if you thought marriage to me a bondage."

A tear slid out from behind her lashes as she lifted them to look into his face. "Oh, Adam! I can't say yes to you— but how am I going to live without you?"

His arms circled her shoulders gently, and his lips touched her temple. "Millicent, have you asked God whether He wants you to stay here?"

She pushed away from him, brushing her hair back from her face. "Do you think because I won't marry you that I'm not committed to God?"

"Not because you. . .you won't marry me."

She steeled herself against the break in his voice.

"You can trust Him never to lead you into a place that's too hard for you, Millicent. He's promised never to leave us or forsake us, but the only way to be happy with Him is to be willing to do anything He asks."

"I *am* committed to Him!"

"I hope you are, Millicent, because I want you to always be happy."

"How dare you accuse me of being out of God's will if I don't marry you!"

"Millicent—"

"I think the rain has let up, Adam." His face told her how much her icy words had hurt him, but she didn't stop him as he put on his hat and coat and went to bring the horse and buggy.

The ride home from Olaf's that evening was long. Adam's clothes were damp and the wind cool, but his insides burned with a fever he was afraid would never burn itself out. He'd never felt so spent, even after a long day in his field. He had needed every ounce of his strength to keep from begging Millicent to stay. If she ever came to him, he wanted her to come freely, with joy shining in her eyes.

"Delight thyself in the Lord, and He shall give thee the desires of thy heart." The verse that had given him strength a few months earlier only increased his pain tonight. Bitterness fueled the fire in his heart. He wanted Millicent beside him through his life. Millicent with her valiant spirit, generous heart, and joy in living. He didn't want to learn how to live without her! What did he care if God had chosen someone else for him? He wanted Millicent.

He jerked Matthew's horse to a sudden halt, and the buggy rocked, sending pyramids of light darting about the road from the swinging lanterns. He buried his face in his hands, and a loud moan mingled with the plunking of rain drops on the buggy's roof. He'd told Millicent the only way to be happy was to commit one's life totally to God, and an hour later he was longing to take control of his own life and hers too. "Lord, forgive me."

The next day Millicent's mind wandered from her teaching and her patience grew thin. Gray skies and scattered showers did nothing for her mood, though they did allow most of the older boys to attend school. The students were rambunctious after their holiday, the younger students eager to tell the older boys everything they had missed. The longing on the older boys' faces as they listened hurt her, and finally, just to keep the others still, she instructed them to write an essay on the Fourth.

By the end of the day she was exhausted from the humid weather and the emotional effort of keeping her thoughts away from Adam, and the day didn't end when classes were over. Millicent had committed herself to tutoring Ellie, beginning that evening.

Together they pulled a bench in front of Millicent's desk so they could share the largest space in the room. Ellie sat down on the bench, her arms wrapped around *The Upper*

Reader, her brown eyes sparkling. "I've hardly been able to sleep since you suggested I study for the teachers' examinations, Miss Strong. Do you really think I can pass?"

"Of course, Ellie. You're intelligent and well-read, one of the best students I've ever taught. The examination is given in September, which gives me plenty of time to help you prepare." She sat down in the chair opposite Ellie. "The counties in this area are all begging for teachers. Why, in Camp Release Township on the other side of the river, they've even hired a thirteen year old boy! I've never heard of a teacher that young."

Ellie lowered her book to her lap, and fear tarnished the sparkle in her eyes. "Do you. . .do you think I'll actually be able to leave home and live with another family?"

"I'm sure of it, Ellie. If you like we can ask Adam . . .Reverend Conrad, that is, or Doctor Strong to let you know of all the openings they hear about on their rounds."

Ellie nodded. "I'd like that." She hesitated before saying shyly, "Thank you for coming up with this plan, Miss Strong. And for agreeing to help me study."

Millicent smiled. "I asked God to help us, Ellie. I think maybe this is His plan."

"Do you really think He cares for us that much, Miss Strong? That He shows us what to do when we're in trouble and everything, I mean?"

"Yes, I do, Ellie—if we're willing to listen to His answers." Guilt flooded her at her words. She felt like a hypocrite. She hadn't the courage to ask God's guidance for herself, to ask whether God wanted her to live in Chippewa City. She pushed the thought away. "Now let's get to work on this plan."

But Millicent's thought continued to stray from the book before them. She wished everything didn't remind her of sacrifice and commitment today! Thor was willing to marry Ellie to keep her from harm, even at the threat to his own future. And the older boys gave up a holiday because they were committed to getting the best education they could. She felt like a shirker. The feeling did not improve her mood.

sixteen

Without Adam's company to look forward to on Saturday evening and Sunday afternoon, the weekend looked too long to spend on the farm. Saturday she rode into town with Stina when the Norwegian woman went for supplies; Millicent would stay with Matthew and Laurina. She had less than two months left here, and she hadn't seen enough of her brother and his family.

But Matthew was out on an emergency when Millicent arrived. She visited with Laurina and the children, though her mind refused to stop thinking of Adam. She helped Laurina with the baking, and read a story to Johnny and Pearl from *The Holiday Album for Girls*, the book she brought Pearl in June. All the while, she was hoping Adam would stop by to see Matthew.

After supper she stood smiling as Johnny and Pearl romped with Mr. Wiggly on the braided rug of the "parlor." Having a family would be nice. Adam would make a good father. The way Johnny and Pearl ran to him whenever they saw him was precious. She loved the way he always knelt or sat beside them, moving down to their level. Her smile died. When Adam did have children of his own, she wouldn't be there to see him loving them.

She enjoyed the family devotions, even without Matthew. Stina and Olaf, though Christians, didn't have a family devotional time. But when the Lindstrom girls whose room she shared saw her reading her Bible each

155

evening, one by one they began to join her.

Matthew still wasn't home by the time the children were tucked in bed. Laurina cut slices of blueberry pie, and the women sat down to the luxury of a visit without children or chores to interrupt them. The windows were open to the evening's cool breeze, and moths thunked against the fly netting, trying to reach the kerosene lamp. The smell of prairie grass drifted in on the breeze and mingled with the odors of kerosene and blueberries.

"Adam may stop by this evening, since he's not going to be at the Lindstroms' visiting you, Millicent. He and Matthew like to play chess together, and Matthew says it's difficult to play at Adam's house now. Adam no longer has the kerosene lamp that hung from the ceiling of his sitting room. He hasn't told Matthew what happened to it, but knowing Adam's generosity, Matthew expects to see it at one of his patients' homes one day." Laurina laughed as she poured coffee into fragile blue and white china cups.

Millicent didn't laugh. Laurina's words jolted her like prairie lightning. "He'll find the lamp in my schoolhouse. Adam didn't tell me it was from his own home."

"Isn't that just like Adam, though." Laurina shook her head, an indulgent smile on her lips. "I've never seen Adam as relaxed as he was with you at the Fourth of July celebration, Millicent. I'm glad you enjoy each other's company. He's such a silent, sober man. It usually takes people a while to feel they know him."

"But he has such speaking eyes."

Laurina's gaze shot across the table. She lowered her coffee cup. "You're very perceptive. It took me almost two years to learn that."

Millicent felt her face flood with warmth.

"Adam isn't a man who gives his heart easily," Laurina said quietly after a moment of silence.

"He gave his heart to you." It hurt to say the words, and her voice was low.

"I'm not so sure."

Millicent looked at her, knowing that the question in her eyes bared her heart to Laurina.

"He never looked at me the way he looks at you, Millicent."

Millicent pushed a piece of pie crust around the blue and white plate, studying it carefully. "We're no longer seeing each other."

When she looked up, she was surprised at the disappointment in Laurina's eyes. "I'm sorry, Millicent. I'd hoped the two of you... I'm sorry."

The longing to tell of Adam's proposal and the subsequent results were strong, but perhaps she would be unfair to Adam if she shared something so personal with the woman he once planned to marry. "Laurina," she said instead, "you were raised in Boston, weren't you?"

"Yes. I lived there with my aunt and uncle from the time I was six until two years ago."

"Don't you miss the conveniences and luxuries of life in Boston?"

A smile lit Laurina's face. "Oh, no. At first I was just so glad to be with my father again. And now there's Matthew." Laurina looked down at her coffee cup and chewed her bottom lip. Her voice was low when she spoke again. "I did miss life in Boston a lot when I moved into the sod house with Johnny and Pearl."

"Adam showed me the sod house. I don't think I would ever have been brave enough to live there."

"Yes, you would," Laurina nodded her head, "if it was the only way to help someone you loved."

Millicent moved to the stove to pour herself another cup of coffee she didn't want, just to avoid Laurina's eyes. "No, I'm not as strong as you are. I don't think I could ever stand to live out here. I want to have my cake and eat it too."

"What do you mean?"

"I don't want to live here, but I want to stay near Matthew."

"And Adam?" When Millicent didn't answer, Laurina said, "I shouldn't have asked. But Matthew would love it if you moved here."

Millicent wrapped a corner of her linen napkin around her finger. "Laurina, how does a person learn to trust God with every part of their life?"

"It's like learning to trust people. The trust grows greater as you get to know Him better and find time and again that He doesn't let you down."

"Yes, I suppose so," Millicent murmured.

Millicent curled up in the rocking chair after Laurina and Matthew were in bed, pulling her knees up beneath her cotton nightgown. The light from the lamp on the table spread mellow rays across her new Bible. She was too restless to sleep. Maybe reading would relax her.

She'd been reading through the Gospel of John, and now, continuing with her plan, she turned to the twelfth chapter, beginning at the twenty-third verse. When she realized the subject of the passage, she was tempted to close the book, but she forced herself to complete the reading.

"And Jesus answered them, saying, 'The hour is come, that the son of man should be glorified.

"'Verily, verily, I say unto you, Except a corn of wheat fall into the ground and die, it abideth alone; but if it die, it bringeth forth much fruit.

"'He that loveth his life shall lose it; and he that hateth his life in this world shall keep it unto life eternal.

"'If any man serve me, let him follow me; and where I am, there shall also my servant be: if any man serve me, him will my Father honour.

"'Now is my soul troubled; and what shall I say? Father, save me from this hour: but for this cause came I unto this hour.'"

Was Adam right? Was it true she wasn't willing to follow Christ completely? Did God think her unworthy because she wouldn't even consider moving to Chippewa City? She was treating God the same way she'd treated Adam, she finally admitted. She wanted Him close, but she wasn't prepared to make sacrifices for Him.

She jumped from the chair and moved restlessly to the window. The stars were fuzzy points of light through the fly netting. An animal cry came through the night, and she shivered: a wolf. The sound was like laughter without joy; here on the edge of the frontier, beneath the beauty of the prairie, the world was a sinister place. Was it any wonder she resisted moving here?

Mr. Wiggly whimpered at her feet, beseeching her with large brown eyes. The wolf must have frightened him also. She picked him up to soothe his trembling, but her thoughts quickly reverted to her dilemma.

Why should love have to sacrifice? She wouldn't want Adam to sacrifice for her. Or God, either.

But they did. The words slipped across her mind. God sacrificed His Son. And Adam risked his life to save her from the runaways when they first met. Thor was willing to sacrifice for Ellie too. And Laurina for Johnny and Pearl.

Christ sacrificed the most. Had He ever questioned what His Father asked of Him? "Now is my soul troubled; and what shall I say? Father, save me from this hour: but for this cause came I unto this hour." She bit her lip. Sacrifice hadn't been easy for Him, either.

Millicent brushed the hair back from her forehead as she sank into the rocking chair again. Was she the only person so selfish that she couldn't sacrifice for someone she loved? She ruffled the pages of her Bible. They flopped open at the violet she had pressed between the pages. Her buffed nail traced the outline of the blossom, one of the violets Adam had picked for her on the way from Granite Falls the day they met. She'd pressed it between the pages of a novel she'd brought along to read on the trip, transferred it later to Adam's Bible, and then to her own to always have it near.

Violets were such beautiful flowers. To make the fragrance she liked to wear, though, their beauty had to be crushed. She would hate to see the fragile blossoms smashed beneath a heavy weight—but otherwise their beauty could not last so long, their fragrance enjoyed where otherwise it would not be known.

Her finger stopped its tracing. Were people the same way? Did the pain of sacrifice only increase their beauty? What would the world be like without people like Adam, Matthew, and Laurina who were willing to sacrifice?

Her tongue flicked across her dry lips. She wanted to be

like those people she admired. "Lord God, I'm sorry I haven't been committed to Thee completely. I'm still not ready to stay here on the prairie, but if it's Thy will that I remain, I ask Thee to change my heart. Whatever Thy desires might be, make Thy desires and my desires one. I'm so weak, Father. Please give me joy in doing Thy will. In Jesus Name, amen."

Would He ask her to live on the frontier? Worse, would He ask her to live here and not marry Adam? She rubbed her chin against the puppy's soft black fur. "I never realized praying could be so scary, Mr. Wiggly."

seventeen

During the following weeks, Millicent threw herself into her work with a vengeance, trying to put Adam out of her mind. She hadn't known it would be like this. She had thought she would miss him at first, but that the pain would fade over time. It didn't. It filled her every waking moment. How foolish she had been to think any comfort of civilization could make up for the love of a man like Adam.

The prairie grass around the schoolhouse grew quickly beneath the summer sun, and the older boys had to cut it often, working in the evening when their other chores were completed. One morning after it was cut, Millicent found that during the night a shelf had been attached to the back wall of the school room, a place to keep the few supplies and books she used. Assuming the shelf was the work of the older boys, she thanked Thorburn, only to find Adam had made the shelf instead.

"Reverend Conrad cut the grass too," Thor told her. "When he found out the older boys were doing it, he offered to cut it for us. He says we need the time to study."

Millicent was too surprised to respond. Thorburn shuffled his large feet, and his sunburned face grew even redder. "The Reverend asks about you whenever I see him, wanting to know if you're well and if there's anything you be needing." He took a deep breath. "Ellie told me she asked you to have him and Young Doc look for a school

162

where she can teach this winter. Seeing how the Reverend cares for you, I told him how it is with Ellie. He says he'll watch out for a place for her."

Millicent's chest ached at Adam's thoughtfulness toward her and Ellie. She longed for the evening to come; then she could be alone in bed, free to let her thoughts go over and over Adam's care of her.

She had only seen him at church services, where she could barely keep her mind on the sermon. Guilt overwhelmed her whenever she saw him, for she knew she was responsible for the pain buried in his eyes. How could she have been so selfish, not telling him from the beginning that she had no intention of staying in Chippewa City once the summer term was over? She'd thought only of her own desires, oblivious to the sorrow she might bring to the kindest man she'd ever known.

She realized now that he had been correct when he suggested she might not be completely committed to God, but at first she hadn't the courage to ask his forgiveness for her anger. When she did muster her courage, he'd left town. He was helping a sister congregation in another township begin work on their new church building; she tried not to envy the people either his presence or their chapel in which to worship.

Meanwhile, the townspeople were excited at the prospect of the library. Millicent met with Mr. Moyer, Mr. Weaver, and a few of the church women to establish rules for the new organization. A person could join for three dollars or by donating a book. A fine of two cents per day was to be assessed for overtime. Perhaps establishing the library was one of God's purposes for bringing her to Chippewa City.

In addition to her regular duties and tutoring Ellie, she spent her evenings coaching her students for their upcoming play, helping them make backdrops and props on their limited funds. When she first suggested putting on the play about the signing of the Declaration of Independence, the students were unsure of their ability.

"Do you really think we can do it, Miss Strong?"

"Of course," she'd encouraged. "With God and each other, you can do anything. Look at the schoolhouse you built." From that point on, they had put their hearts and souls into the preparation, for the funds they raised would be used to buy more school books.

They were wonderful children. She would miss them terribly when she left—and only two weeks remained in the term. Soon the older boys would be helping with the harvest. Purple asters and towering sunflowers brightened the prairie now, and she wondered with a pang of regret what flora the changing landscape would display after she went back East.

Ellie was doing well with her studies for the teachers' examination, and so far her father hadn't hit her again. Millicent prayed daily that his temper would hold until Ellie was out of the house. The solution wasn't perfect, but it was at least a beginning.

The first Friday in August dawned hazy and hot. As the day wore one, gray clouds tinged with yellow piled high in rolling masses. The air was thick and unusually still.

The unstable weather affected the children, who were restless and abnormally inattentive all day. Millicent finally gave up the class work and let the children work on the play.

Thor arrived late in the morning as his father said it was too uncomfortable to work in the fields. Thor brought with him a large kettle and a bushel of sweet corn. Millicent agreed to a picnic lunch, and the corn was boiled over a fire in the school yard. She thought she had never tasted anything as good as that corn with Stina's butter melted over the golden kernels. Wild grapes and plums the Lindstroms had gathered from near the river were a perfect ending to the simple meal.

When the children went outside for recess, she was dismayed to see Charley riding into the school yard, swaying in his saddle, his arm still in a sling from his tumble on the Fourth of July. He was singing at the top of his lungs, and it wasn't a song for students' ears, or a teacher's either.

With fists propped on her hips, she waited for him to come to a stop beside her. He leaned over in his saddle, with his one good hand clutching the horn to keep his seat. "Hi, sweet thing."

His breath nearly knocked her over. She was aware of the students staring at them. Some of them snickered, but most were horrified.

"I believe you've lost your way, Mr. Bender," she said in her most commanding teacher's manner. "This is a schoolhouse, not a saloon." Where had he found the liquor? Two weeks earlier, the citizens had voted Chippewa City dry.

His lopsided grin revealed his yellow teeth. "Want I should teach these little varmints somethin'?"

If she were a man, she would send him out of here so fast he'd be reeling for weeks! "The students don't need to learn how to drink intoxicating liquors, Mr. Bender."

"Aw, call me Charley, will ya, Millie?" He leaned closer to her, and almost fell from his saddle. His horse snorted and danced as Charley tried to right himself.

Thor stepped up beside her. "Do you want me to get rid of him for you, Miss Strong?"

"Thank you, Thor, but I'd prefer if you took the children to another part of the yard and involved them in something else. A game of baseball perhaps. That should keep their attention while I deal with Mr. Bender."

"Yes, ma'am. But just yell if you need my help." He kept his steady gaze on Charley as he called the kids and gathered them to pick teams.

Charley finally had himself seated upright again, and he brought his dancing bay back to Millicent. "Heard ya finally listened to my advice and gave the Reverend the heave-ho." His grin made her skin crawl. "Bet you jest been waitin' for me to call."

She crossed her arms over her chest, itching to punch him in his big red nose. Even if etiquette allowed a woman to do such a thing, though, God would probably disapprove, she thought. "You lose your bet, Mr. Bender. I would appreciate it if you'd leave. I have students to teach."

"Now, Millie, is that any way to treat a gentleman who rides all the way out on this lonesome prairie, riskin' life and limb, jest to ask you to go to a dance? There's goin' to be a humdinger of a dance at Granite Falls this Saturday night. Bet you'd be the prettiest filly there."

She took a deep breath. "I can't tell you how thrilling it is to be compared to a horse, Mr. Bender. But even with such an inducement, I find I must decline your invitation. I—"

A clap of thunder drowned the rest of her sentence, and sent Charley's bay up on its powerful hind legs. Charley slid ungracefully off, and the bay took off toward Stina and Olaf's at a hard gallop, its rein streaming behind it

Disgusted, Millicent watched the bay leave; what was she going to do with Charley now that his conveyance was gone? She and the students walked back to the school. She looked over her shoulder to see Charley struggling unsuccessfully to get to his feet. The combination of liquor and a broken arm were too much for his balancing abilities. Reluctantly, Millicent went back to help him.

He smelled worse than ever. She gasped at the heavy wave of liquor-filled air that hit her, as Charley reached for his back pocket with his good hand. "Look what that good-for-nothing plug did this time. Broke my bottle."

"He should have broken it hours ago, Mr. Bender." Millicent reached down to assist him, but suddenly she dropped his arm. She jerked straight as a fence post, staring at the sky. A black spinning tail had dropped from the clouds. "Help us, God!"

The children! She dashed toward them, picking up her binding skirts, hating the high-heeled shoes that made running so difficult. Where could the children be safe? The flat prairie had no where to hide. The root cellar! Was there time? She screamed for Thor as she glanced over her shoulder at the funnel. It was already three times the size it was when she spotted it. She could see the dust dance where the funnel met the ground.

"Thor!" She pointed toward the funnel as she ran. He turned in the direction of her arm. Terror drove the color from his broad face and turned his muscled body to stone.

Millicent slid to a stop in front of him, grabbing his arm.

"The root cellar, Thor! We have to get the children to the root cellar!"

He revived instantly, spurred by the directions that gave hope. Together they gathered the children, who needed no prodding when they saw the tornado. Rain was falling by the time they reached the door, great, pelting drops mixed with hail and driven by a vicious wind that tried to grab the door from Thor's hands. Darkness thick as night fell over them, filled with the cries and screams of the children. Millicent could no longer see how close the tornado was. She pushed the children inside the cellar as Thor struggled with the door. When the last child was inside, she had to scream into Thor's ear to make herself heard. "Get in the cellar, Thor! I'm going for Charley!"

"No!" He hurled the word as he grabbed for her, but he missed; she stood just out of his reach, yelling above the storm, "Save the children, Thor!"

Then she was running toward the schoolhouse, buffeted by the winds that dragged at her skirt and hair. She looked back once and thanked God when she saw the shadow of Thor disappear behind the closing root cellar door. Knowing the children were safe renewed her strength, and she pushed against the wind to reach Charley. He had finally made it to his feet, but he hadn't the coordination to walk against the winds.

Where was the twister? From the winds and noise, it must be almost on them. "He's promised to never leave us or forsake us." Adam's words about Jesus flooded her mind. She tugged at Charley's good arm with both her hands, hair whipping across her face, her soaked skirts dragging at her legs. Thou must help me, God, she cried silently. Charley doesn't know Thee!

They hadn't a chance of reaching the root cellar or the schoolhouse. The most protection they could hope for was the fire ditch left at the edge of the school yard. Millicent pulled Charley down with her behind the small ridge of dirt, pushing their bodies against the side of the ditch nearest the direction where she'd last seen the tornado. Even the ground seemed to rumble and groan.

A moment later, the winds tore at her legs and skirt as though the very air had hands, grasping at her, trying to pull her from the earth. She thought her hair would be yanked from her head. She tried to dig her face into the dirt, her fingers aching from her hold on Charley. Was she going to smother from the black soil and the pressure?

She could feel dirt and debris strike her body—and then her head seemed to explode. Her hands loosened their hold on Charley. As she sank into the darkness, her mind cried out to God. Save the children!

eighteen

Adam lifted his black hat and wiped his forearm across his brow as looked up at the roiling clouds. Miserable day. Hot and humid and not the hint of a breeze to cool a man down. His gaze dropped to his mule, plodding faithfully away in front of the creaking wagon, her hooves thudding dully against the ground. Not a fit day for a beast, either. "Never mind, Butternut, only a little over a mile and we'll be at the schoolhouse. You can get a nice cool drink there while you rest."

And he could see Millicent. Would she be angry if he stopped? The students would still be there when he arrived, and if his presence upset her, they would be a buffer until he watered Butternut and left. He hadn't talked with her since the night he asked her to marry him. The night she refused.

Not that he didn't want to talk to her, but he hadn't received any encouragement when they'd shaken hands and exchanged greetings after services. At least she was attending church and the new Sunday School. He'd been afraid at first that her pride and anger would keep her away from Sabbath services.

Only a couple more weeks, and she'd be returning to Illinois. The thought left his stomach churning like the clouds above his head. How could he stand never to see her again? But she was right; he couldn't leave Chippewa

City, not until he felt God wanted him to move on. He'd asked God a dozen times over the last weeks to reveal to him if this were the time, but he hadn't received an answer—no hunches, no calls from other churches. Nothing. Just a hunger to be near Millicent, and he didn't trust that as an answer.

He needed all his strength to stay away from her. He wanted to beg her to stay, but he knew that even if she agreed, they wouldn't be happy together, not unless they were both committed completely to Christ.

A hint of breeze touched his face, and he looked up in surprise. "Looks like that rain that's been threatening all day might finally start, Butternut." He'd welcome the rain, but he would like to get to the protection of the school-house first. Of course, he could stop at Olaf's instead, but then he wouldn't see Millicent. He could just make out the small schoolhouse in the distance. Now, if the rain would hold off a few more minutes—

His heart froze within him as a black wisp of cloud off to his right dove to the earth, spinning like a top, and headed across the unbroken land toward the schoolhouse. He leaned forward and whipped the reins across Butternut's flank. She leaped forward in bewilderment and fear at the unusual lashing. "Come on, Butternut! We have to warn them!"

But he knew in his heart it was too late. Drops were beating about them now. A moment later the winds and rains lashed at them, and Butternut began cutting a diagonal path as the storm blew her and the wagon from the rutted path that served as a road. Adam's hat lifted from his head and tumbled along the top of the chest-high prairie grass, bent now almost to the ground. His eyes burned from the dust and rain as he tried to keep the growing, whirling funnel in sight through the sudden darkness. The twister was bearing down on the schoolhouse now. Every inch of his being screamed to God, but his terror for Millicent and the students was too great to form his prayer into words.

Butternut almost pulled his arms from their sockets in her fear, but he kept her headed toward the schoolhouse. And then the twister had passed the school yard, continuing its rampage across the land.

Was the schoolhouse still there? He couldn't tell through the rain. They raced closer, and his stomach felt suddenly hollow. The school and outbuildings were gone. Nothing but shredded timber covered the land. Could anyone have possibly lived through such destruction?

He pulled Butternut to a stop and climbed down from the wagon, looking about him, dazed. Where should he begin? "God, show me what to do." He brushed away the rain that covered his face and realized it was mixed with tears.

Incredibly, he saw a heap of timber and plaster move. He rushed toward it, impatient with the rubble that impeded him. The root cellar door was trying to lift; joy gave him added strength as he pushed and tossed the debris. "Hold on! I need to clear off the door before you can open it!" he called to those imprisoned below. He could hear Thor call back to him, letting him know they were all right, while sobs from the younger students drifted through the pile of rubble. Thank God for the root cellar! One of the few places on the prairie a twister couldn't find them. His chest felt suddenly clean with relief.

Sobbing students rushed from the black hole when he finally threw back the door. They stumbled into the debris-scattered yard, blinking against the rain-soaked daylight, hanging onto each other for balance and strength. Thor grasped Adam's arm in his large hand. "Have you seen Miss Strong?"

Adam's blood turned to ice. "She isn't with you?"

Thor shook his head and quickly told him how Millicent had tried to save Charley. Adam held a trembling hand across his face to hold back his pain and fear. "God, please let her be alive," he whispered as he searched the torn landscape. He turned to Thor and saw the young Norwegian trying to make out his father's farm through the rain. "Your family should be fine. The tornado didn't touch your farm." Thor's shoulders relaxed.

Adam asked Ellie to calm the younger students while he and Thor began searching for Millicent and Charley. As minutes passed and they found no sign of them, resentment began to rise in Adam's chest. The drunken man was responsible for Millicent not reaching the safety of the root cellar. Adam had almost given up hope when a feeble cry for help reached his ears. Then a splintered timber moved, and a man's arm in a ragged sleeve poke into view. Adam headed toward it like a wild man, Thor right behind him.

They soon had a sobbing Charley freed. He sputtered in a drunken slur, "If it weren't for tryin' to save me, Miss Millicent would be okay." Adam wanted to shake him until his yellow teeth rattled. "She was right beside me, Preacher, pulling me down into that prairie fire ditch, and then the world turned upside down on us!"

Adam tore at the rubble beside them. If Millicent had

been with Charley when the twister— Thor grabbed at his sleeve. "Reverend, we've got to go slow! If Miss Strong is under there, we don't want to hurt her more."

He tried to slow down, and Thor helped him drag the broken boards and plaster aside. At last they saw a blue and rose striped skirt, and a sob of thanksgiving escaped Adam's throat. If only she were alive!

Moments later they were able to pull her out of the wreckage. Blood from a gash on the back of her head covered her hair and face. Adam stopped breathing as he held her limp wrist, feeling for a pulse. "She's alive, Thor!"

"Thank God!"

Adam pressed his handkerchief against the wound to stop the bleeding. He wished Charley would stop his whimpering. He'd never felt such contempt for a man.

The rain began to revive Millicent, and she moaned, wincing before her eyes even opened. Then the blonde-tipped lashes lifted slowly, and she looked into his eyes, squinting. "Adam?"

"It's okay, Millicent. It's over."

A frown furrowed the forehead over her pain-glazed eyes. "Is. . .is that the children crying?"

The weakness of her voice frightened him. "Just from nerves. They're all fine. You saved them, Millicent."

Her fingers touched his sleeve. "Charley. Where is Charley?"

"He's right here. He's fine."

"He needs to know about Jesus, Adam."

His teeth clenched. The man almost got her killed, and she was thinking about his relationship with God.

Her fingers clutched at his shirt. "You'll tell him, won't you? About Jesus?"

He swallowed hard. "Yes."

She gave a little sigh. "It's all right then." Her hand slipped from his arm.

nineteen

Two days later she awoke in bed at Stina and Olaf's farm. Adam and Matthew were in the room with her, and from the look of the scruffy beard on Matthew's face and the gray circles beneath Adam's eyes, she knew they had been there ever since she was brought to the farm from the school yard.

"Gave us quite a scare, Millie." She could see that in spite of his smile, Matthew was still scared for her.

Her first words were to question again the safety of the children and Charley. After being assured they were all alive and well, she relaxed. Matthew sent Adam from the room so he could examine her. When he was through, he grinned. "Even a Minnesota twister can't stop a Strong."

She smiled feebly back at him. "Can I talk to Adam now?"

"Only for a minute. He's itching to talk to you too."

The relief in Adam's eyes when he stood beside her bed made her shy. "Matthew says you'll be fine."

"Yes. He told me you were the one who found me. Thank you for saving my life—once again." The words seemed so inadequate.

Adam knelt beside the bed and took her hand in his. "I've never been so scared, seeing that twister hit and thinking there was no chance you and the children would make it through alive."

He brought her hand to his lips, and the sweetness of his touch after all these weeks made her lips tremble. "I thought you would hate me," she whispered. "You made no effort to see me after. . . ."

"After you refused to marry me."

She couldn't meet his eyes. "Yes."

He slipped a finger beneath her chin and gently urged her face upward. She dared a timid glance at his eyes. "I could never hate you, Millicent. It would be like hating myself." How could such a deep voice be so gentle, she wondered. "You were too tempting to be near, Millicent. I was afraid I would beg you to stay—or I would decide to go just so we could be together. I couldn't hear God's voice over my desire for you."

Millicent took a shaky breath. She wanted to throw herself into his arms, but his words encouraged her to tell him what she had planned to before the tornado. "Adam, I promised myself I would tell you this at the first opportunity. You were right about me. I wasn't completely committed to God. I thought I was, but I learned I was holding parts of my life back from Him." She saw the hope leap in his ebony eyes, and she looked down at the blanket, plucking at it with her free hand. "I don't know what He wishes me to do with my life yet. I'm not sure whether He'll ask me to stay in Chippewa City. But I've asked Him to show me His will."

She was afraid her words would hurt him. She couldn't tell him she would marry him and stay in Chippewa City, because she didn't know herself. But when she dared look at him again, his eyes were warm and smiling. "I already knew you had committed your life to Him."

Her mouth opened slightly in surprise. "How could you know that?"

"Because you performed the most Christ-like act possible. You risked your life for Charley."

"I couldn't just let him die."

He squeezed her hand. "I know. You made me promise to tell him about Christ, after he almost got you killed. First I had to forgive him. When I thought of the danger he exposed you to—" The anguish in his eyes and voice caught at her heart. "God forgive me for my evil thoughts toward that man." He took a long ragged breath.

"Charley has repented and asked for God's salvation. He says if God can give a little lady like you the spunk to save a drunken fool like him, he thinks he'd better give Him a try."

"I'm so glad!" She was humbled to realize God had actually used her to show another person their need of Him. "Were any farms destroyed by the tornado?"

"No. Some crops were destroyed, and Ellie's father lost his barn and some cattle."

"Is. . .is there anything left of the schoolhouse?"

"Nothing. Not a board."

Tears pooled in her eyes. "After all the children's work. They must be so discouraged." Through her tears, she saw her pain reflected in Adam's eyes.

Although Millicent was eager to get back to work, Matthew insisted she rest for a few more days, as she was still weak from shock and loss of blood. She reluctantly agreed, but only after arranging with Ellie to teach the classes while she recovered. Matthew and Laurina agreed the students could use the sod house for a school temporarily. Millicent gave Ellie money to buy a few books from the mercantile to replace those lost in the tornado. The students would have to share, but she didn't want them kept from their studies so close to the final examinations.

A week later, Matthew drove an impatient Millicent over to the soddie in his buggy. The school day was almost over, for Matthew insisted she not begin work yet, but she could barely wait to see the students and find out for herself how they were doing under Ellie's teaching. Her heart contracted as they drove into the yard. The old schoolhouse would have seemed elegant compared to the sod building.

Anders was standing and reciting his sums when they entered. Upon seeing her in the doorway, he stopped and all the students stood. Ellie's eyes met hers with a glad light. "Continue, Anders," Millicent said, and the other students took their seats as he picked up his recitation.

Millicent's eyes examined the room while Ander's voice droned on through the eight-times-eights to the twelve-times-twelves. The whitewashed walls had been recently cleaned. A simple painted blackboard stood against one wall. The table she remembered from the night Adam asked her to marry him was now Ellie's desk, and the crude bench her chair. New muslin curtains hung at the windows on either side of the door, fresh wooden planks covered the floor, and the stove had been cleaned until it shone.

The smell of new wood mingled with the damp earthen smell of the soddie. Millicent was surprised to see that the students were seated on three long benches made of newly planed lumber. More surprising still was the stack of slates and the pile of new readers and history books on Ellie's desk, far more than the money she'd given Ellie could have bought. Crisp new maps hung on the walls. Where had it all come from?

When Anders completed his sums, Ellie dismissed the students for the day. They rushed to surround Millicent, asking after her health, telling her about their past week, all of them speaking at once. Their fondness for her touched her heart, and she smiled at them through misty eyes. She had no desire to ask any of them to be still—until the word "play" caught her attention. She hadn't even thought about the play! She caught Ellie's eye. "The play? Wasn't everything destroyed in the storm?"

The students hushed as Ellie answered. "Most of the scripts were blown away, and the props too. But Lars had one script at home, and most of us know our parts already. We can make do with less scenery and props than we planned. Miss Bartlett from the Chippewa City school said we can use her school for the performance. I. . .I thought you wouldn't mind. We want to use the money we raise to pay for the new schoolbooks and everything."

Millicent lowered herself to one of the new benches. "Mind? I'm so proud of you all I could burst."

A combination of pride and embarrassment filled Ellie's face. "We'd like to dedicate the performance to you, Miss Strong. You told us that 'with God and each other we can do anything.' You were right. We even survived the tornado together."

The children's faces swam before her as tears filled her

eyes. Her voice was wobbly when she said, "You are the best class any teacher ever had the privilege of teaching. You've blessed my life beyond measure."

Anders leaned against the bench beside her. "Miss Strong, I wish you could stay and be our teacher again."

Murmurs of assent filled the room. "Me, too," Ellie agreed.

"Thank you, but I have to ask God what He wants me to do."

"Oh. Well, is it okay if I ask Him to let you stay?" Anders asked.

She caught back a laugh. "I think it would be better if you asked Him to help me do whatever He wants."

"Okay. But I hope He wants you to stay."

She rubbed a hand lightly across his small shoulders. "Thank you, Anders."

Slowly, the students left, until only Ellie, Matthew, and Millicent were left. Millicent and Ellie were busy discussing examination plans when they heard the jangling and creaking of a wagon. A minute later, Millicent stopped speaking in mid-sentence as Adam stopped in the doorway. His eyes found hers immediately, and the look in them made her feel she was wrapped in his arms.

Matthew cleared his throat. "May I drop you at home, Miss Brandt?" Millicent's gaze darted to her brother's face, but he only grinned at her. "I think my sister has found another way home."

Ellie smiled widely over her shoulder at Millicent as she and Matthew left.

"Do you mind if I see you home, Millicent?"

"No. I'm glad to see you, Adam." She wanted to tell him

to never feel unwelcome in her presence but she hadn't the courage. They stared at each other in uncomfortable silence.

Adam removed his hat, dropping it on one of the new benches as he moved slowly across the room to Millicent. Her heart hammered so that she was certain it was louder than Butternut's hooves against the prairie roads. He stopped a yard away from her. "I think I've found a school for Ellie, if she passes the teachers' examinations next month."

His neutral topic made Millicent's breath release in a rush. "Ellie?"

He nodded. "In the next county, Lac Qui Parle. There's a lack of teachers there, also."

Millicent looked around the small room. What would happen to the students if she left? Would they have any classes next year? "I've worried and prayed for the students all week, Adam. It must have been awful to lose the school for which they'd worked so hard. I hated that schoolhouse the first time I saw it—but when I remembered it this week, all I could see was a symbol of the students' love for knowledge. I thought it was dreadful they were coming here for classes. But all this—" She spread her arms to take in the refurbished room. "Where did it all come from?"

"Others furnished the supplies, but the students did the cleaning, made the blackboard and benches, and laid the floor."

She moved to one of the new benches and sat down, her purple skirt lying in graceful folds around her. "I've been so foolish, Adam. I thought civilization was made up of architecture and comforts. Now I know it's not that at all. It's the way people treat each other, the way they love each other."

His eyes didn't leave her face. He didn't move a muscle.

"When I came here, I saw Chippewa City as a handful of crude buildings in the midst of the wilderness. But Chippewa City is the people who live in it and around it: Matthew and Laurina, and the school children—and you, Adam." His name was barely a whisper.

His eyes darkened, and she saw his hands clench at his side, but still he didn't move or speak.

"I want the people here to have better lives, Adam. I want Ellie to get her teaching certificate, and the children to have better schools, and the town to have a good library. I want to be part of their lives. I guess. . .I guess God wants me to be a part of the frontier after all."

He was beside her in two long steps, straddling the bench next to her. A twinkle formed deep in his brown eyes. "I don't think God plans to make you *part* of the frontier, Millicent. I think He plans to use you to help *end* the frontier, to civilize it."

She bit her bottom lip hard. "And you, Adam. Do you have plans for me?"

Adam rubbed his hands over his thighs. His lips became a tight line. "I have nothing to offer you, Millicent."

Her heart split at his harsh tone. "I. . .I see." So God wanted her to teach here without marrying Adam after all. Was she strong enough. "Do you. . .still love Laurina?"

His hand cupped her cheek and turned her face to his. "No." He reached into his pocket and pulled out a worn and folded newspaper clipping. "The day before we met,

I read a letter to the editor from a school ma'am. I remember wishing I could meet her."

Millicent touched the paper with a trembling finger. "You kept it?"

"Yes, and once I realized you wrote it, I kept it with me always." He trailed a finger across her cheek, and she shivered from his touch. "It's not for lack of loving you that I can't marry you, Millicent." His thumb traced the line of her jaw, and his urgent voice became soft. "It's most certainly not for lack of love."

Hope flickered in her chest. "What is it then, Adam?"

She could see the struggle in his face as he battled with himself. His palms rode down his thighs and back again. "The church owns my home, Millicent, and the bank owns everything else. I mortgaged my field, my tools, my wagon, even Butternut." His palms faced the ceiling as he shrugged helplessly. "The students. . .they needed so much. . .and now all I have to offer you is debt. The students' parents have offered to pay me back, when they can afford it. If the harvests are good. . . ."

"You placed yourself in debt for the school?" she asked slowly. "But what about the church? They haven't even a sod house of their own."

"I spoke with the elders before going to the bank. They understood and agreed with my decision."

He'd mortgaged everything for the students she loved. She could barely take it in. His heart was as wide as the prairie. "Mr. Weaver said married women can teach in this state, Adam." His lips parted in protest, but she placed two gloved fingers over them. "And I have a little capital in a bank back in Illinois."

He caught her wrist and pulled her hand from his face. "I know how important it is to you to keep your capital separate from your husband's when you marry."

"You've given your own capital to the school and children who are so dear to my heart. I should like all I have to be yours."

He caught his breath at her words, and she saw the conflict in his eyes; he longed for her, yet he dreaded dragging her into debt. "Isn't that as it should be, Adam?" she beseeched quietly. "The joining of all that we have and all that we are, to be used in God's service? 'With one mind and one mouth glorifying God.'"

Adam's arms slipped around her waist and drew her against his chest. His lips touched her temple, and his deep voice trembled. "Yes, my love. That's as it should be."

She sighed and snuggled deeper into his arms. She'd thought she would never experience their warmth again. "You won't mind if I teach after we're married, then? If you've found another assignment for Ellie, the students here will need an instructor."

He didn't answer at first, and she wondered at his hesitation. His chin rubbed across her hair, catching her curls. When he spoke, his voice quivered. "Until we have children of our own, Millicent?"

Their own children. The thought made her hurt with longing. She nodded, her cheek against his shirt.

"Are you sure you won't be sorry you gave up the East for life with a dull preacher?"

Millicent could hear the fear in his husky whisper. Her hands slipped behind his neck as she lifted her head from his chest. She wanted him to see for herself the joy his love gave her. "Oh, yes, Adam, I'm sure. To quote a certain school ma'am, 'Who would go to the cities of the East when such inducements are held forth on the frontier?'"

A Letter To Our Readers

Dear Reader:

In order that we might better contribute to your reading enjoyment, we would appreciate your taking a few minutes to respond to the following questions. When completed, please return to the following:

Karen Carroll, Editor
Heartsong Presents
P.O. Box 719
Uhrichsville, Ohio 44683

1. Did you enjoy reading *The Unfolding Heart*?
   ☐ Very much. I would like to see more books by this author!
   ☐ Moderately
   I would have enjoyed it more if _____

   _____

2. Are you a member of *Heartsong Presents*? Yes   No
   If no, where did you purchase this book? _____

   _____

3. What influenced your decision to purchase this book? (Circle those that apply.)

Cover	Back cover copy
Title	Friends
Publicity	Other _____

4. On a scale from 1 (poor) to 10 (superior), please rate the following elements.

___Heroine   ___Plot

___Hero   ___Inspirational theme

___Setting   ___Secondary characters

5. What settings would you like to see covered in *Heartsong Presents* books?

_____

_____

6. What are some inspirational themes you would like to see treated in future books?_____

_____

_____

7. Would you be interested in reading other *Heartsong Presents* titles?   Yes   No

8. Please circle your age range:

| Under 18 | 18-24 | 25-34 |
| 35-45 | 46-55 | Over 55 |

9. How many hours per week do you read? _____

Name _____

Occupation _____

Address _____

City _____ State _____ Zip _____

...... Hearts♥ng ......

Great Inspirational Romance at a Great Price!

Heartsong Presents books are inspirational romances in contemporary and historical settings, designed to give you an enjoyable, spirit-lifting reading experience. You can choose from 52 wonderfully written titles from some of today's best authors like Collen Reecé, Jacquelyn Cook, Yvonne Lehman, and many others.

HEARTSONG PRESENTS TITLES AVAILABLE NOW:

(If ordering from this page, please remember to include it with the order form.)

·········Presents·········

ABOVE TITLES ARE $2.95 EACH

LOVE A GREAT LOVE STORY?

Introducing Heartsong Presents —
                                    Your Inspirational Book Club

Heartsong Presents Christian romance reader's service will provide you with four never before published romance titles every month! In fact, your books will be mailed to you at the same time advance copies are sent to book reviewers. You'll preview each of these new and unabridged books before they are released to the general public.

These books are filled with the kind of stories you have been longing for—stories of courtship, chivalry, honor, and virtue. Strong characters and riveting plot lines will make you want to read on and on. Romance is not dead, and each of these romantic tales will remind you that Christian faith is still the vital ingredient in an intimate relationship filled with true love and honest devotion.

Sign up today to receive your first set. Send no money now. We'll bill you only $9.97 post-paid with your shipment. Then every month you'll automatically receive the latest four "hot off the press" titles for the same low post-paid price of $9.97. That's a savings of 50% off the $4.95 cover price. When you consider the exaggerated shipping charges of other book clubs, your savings are even greater!

THERE IS NO RISK—you may cancel at any time without obligation. And if you aren't completely satisfied with any selection, return it for an immediate refund.

TO JOIN, just complete the coupon below, mail it today, and get ready for hours of wholesome entertainment.

Now you can curl up, relax, and enjoy some great reading full of the warmhearted spirit of romance.